Also by

Shannon Esposito

SAHARA'S SONG

STRANGE NEW FEET

THE MONARCH

KARMA'S A BITCH

LADY LUCK RUNS OUT

SILENCE IS GOLDEN

For Pete's Sake

(A Pet Psychic Mystery No.4)

A NOVEL

Shannon Esposito

misterio press

For Pete's Sake
(A Pet Psychic Mystery No.4)

Copyright © Shannon Esposito, 2016
Published by misterio press

Printed in The United States of America

* * * * *

Visit Shannon Esposito's official website at
www.murderinparadise.com

* * * * *

Cover Art by Isabelle Arné
Indiadrummond.com

Formatting by Debora Lewis
arenapublishing.org

* * * * *

ISBN-13: 978-0-9908747-9-9

For my sweet friend, Roxanne,
whose light we miss dearly.

CHAPTER ONE

Peter Vanek leaned on his desk, doting over the set of flattened out construction plans under his palms. They were his dream transformed into lines, shades and numbers. His eyes burned as a sudden rush of emotion overwhelmed him.

Gratitude? Yes, gratitude. But also awe.

He'd never cared much about money. He had a modest house for St. Pete standards, a photography business he'd built from scratch with nothing but hustle, sweat and a never-stop-learning attitude. What he did care about was his reputation, his health and saving as many animals as he could while he was on this planet. And Bianca ... now that she'd said yes.

He'd prayed for a miracle and he'd received one. Not in the way he'd expected, but still, he couldn't deny the serendipity that would now allow him to turn this dream on paper into a concrete reality. In one moment, his life had changed. By one single coincidence. One gift dropped in his lap by the universe.

Who knew, when he'd agreed to take the job, that it would lead to this? Miracle was too small a word.

Did he feel guilty? Sure, a twinge maybe. But he just had to remind himself he wasn't hurting anyone—people bring on their own pain—and so many more lives would be saved. Sometimes the ends really do justify the means.

"Well, today is the day," he whispered to his empty office as he carefully rolled up the plans, something he'd done a hundred times in the last two years. He checked the time on his phone, slipped it back into his slacks pocket and then strolled into the kitchen.

"All done, kiddo?" Squatting with a grin, he gave the Yorkie puppy a quick scratch beneath the chin, then picked up the empty food bowl and rinsed it out in the sink. Finally he made his own breakfast by juicing kale, carrots and apples.

After finishing his drink and cleaning up the juicer, he checked the time again. Light wings of excitement fluttered in his chest. The world seemed brighter. Full of possibility and hope. Time to get ready to go.

Moving into the bedroom with the tiny brown and black puppy at his heels, he slipped into his tux jacket and checked his reflection in the bathroom mirror. It was going to be a stifling hot Florida morning—the kind that feels like you just stuck your face in an oven—much too hot to be stuffed into a tux, but he prided himself on looking professional so there wasn't really a choice. After straightening out his bowtie, he moved to finish the last item on his to-do list—one final check of his equipment.

"What'd you think, kiddo? About that time?" He glanced over at the puppy chasing its tiny stub of a tail in circles and chuckled. "You're just trying your hardest to get me to keep you around, aren't you? Here's a secret … it just might be working."

On his way out of the bedroom, he stopped to look at the framed photos on his dresser. He smiled fondly at the one of him and Bianca. This was definitely shaping up to be the best year of his life.

A light knock sounded from the front of the house.

His gaze froze on the puppy, who'd stopped spinning and now watched him with his miniature head cocked quizzically.

His heart began to beat like a jackhammer.

Was this the answer to his prayers? He wasn't a betting man, but if he was ... he'd bet on yes.

CHAPTER TWO

Every bride wants her wedding to be perfect, a day to remember. A fairytale. But, in the case of my best friend and business partner Sylvia's wedding, today included a missing-in-action wedding photographer and a not-so-happy mother of the bride.

I chewed on a cuticle as I surveyed the long faces in the posh Vinoy Resort suite. There was Sylvia, me—the maid of honor—and Sylvia's three bridesmaid cousins. We were all running out of ways to keep her from having a meltdown.

Think, Darwin.

Then I clapped my hands. "I know! Y'all have phone cameras so we can just take some pictures of each other until the photographer gets here."

I was trying unsuccessfully to stop the red hives that were creeping up Sylvia's neck, beneath her beaded lace plunging neckline. Panic was threatening to kick off its shoes and make itself at home in her psyche.

Sylvia moaned and dabbed the Kleenex under her eye, where a tear of frustration had slipped. Shaking her head, she twisted her engagement ring with nervous energy.

"You don't understand, *mi amiga*. My mother ... I already had to beg her for her blessing and promise her we'd get our children baptized. She gave in reluctantly, but she's still upset about us not getting married by the church. *Anything* that goes wrong now, she'll take as a sign she was mistaken to give her blessing. A sign that God doesn't actually approve and our marriage will be cursed if we go through with it."

I knew my mouth was hanging open. I even heard my own mother's voice saying, "Darwin, shut your mouth before you swallow a fly." I couldn't move, though.

Cursed? How can anyone look at the love between Sylvia and Landon and ever think they'd be cursed?

This was not good. We had to do something. I hopped off of the bed and dug through my bag for my cell phone.

"I have an idea. I'll call Charlie and see if she can come take some photos. She was taking lessons from the wedding photographer, remember? He was teaching her how to photograph shelter dogs. She just got a new camera."

Sylvia actually cracked a smile. "Shelter dogs?"

Sylvia's three cousins, however, were not amused. They whirled in their red Vera Wang bridesmaid dresses and stared with undisguised horror. Then they converged on Sylvia like a flock of birds and began soothing her in Portuguese, comforting her with pats and shoulder squeezes while shooting me sharp, disapproving glances.

Good job, Darwin. Way to ostracize yourself some more.

I sighed and made the call. Luckily Charlie was close by.

"The other photographer will be here in less than ten minutes."

While we waited for someone who knew what they were doing, I decided to take a few photos myself. I framed the women on the screen of my camera phone and clicked. I captured three unamused faces and Sylvia's sad stare. I gave up and refilled my glass with the complementary orange juice mimosa. Breakfast of champions on your friend's wedding day, especially when things are unraveling.

Charlie arrived at our room fairly quickly. I barely recognized her without her usual skinny jeans and some kind of funky hat. Instead she was wearing a sky-blue sundress and white leather sandals. Her dyed-pink hair was pinned to one side with a dragonfly barrette. Charlie was the veterinarian technician student we'd hired to help us out at Darwin's Pet Boutique back in December, during snowbird season. She had a heart of gold and had grown to be one of my favorite people on the planet. Especially at the moment.

"Charlie! Thank the stars you're here." I pulled her quickly through the door and deeper into the room, introducing her to the cousins.

She looked a bit overwhelmed as they all talked at once. Or should I say, vented their frustration all at once? Breaking free, she finally made her way to the other side of the queen-sized bed to give Sylvia a careful hug.

"Wow, you look like you just stepped out of Bridal Magazine. That dress is to-die-for gorgeous."

Sylvia barely managed a thank you.

"Hey, chin up, buttercup. I'm sure Pete has a really good reason for being late. He's a good guy and wouldn't stand you up like this on purpose. He's probably on his way right now. Meanwhile, no worries. I got this." She popped the lens cap off her fancy digital camera and moved to pull open the thick blinds, letting the soft morning light pour in. "We can get some good shots in here. Pete taught me all about utilizing natural lighting. I'll just use a little fill flash for the shadows. If he comes, he can take over. If not, you'll still have some first-rate photos. Promise."

I caught a whiff of the sweet scent of roses as she retrieved Sylvia's giant red bouquet off the round table in the corner and brought it to her.

"Girls, come pile in behind Sylvia on the bed. No wait." She pointed to Sylvia's shortest cousin. "Lizete, you go ahead and stand beside her and rest your hand on her shoulder." She adjusted Sylvia's dress, fanning it out in front of her until the sequins glittered in the sunlight. Then she adjusted the way we were sitting so we were angled more sideways to the camera. "Beautiful, girls."

I felt my own shoulders unglue themselves from my ears as I began to relax under Charlie's guidance. Thank the stars she came so quickly. I wanted to ring that photographer's neck for stressing Sylvia out like this. Not very professional at all.

We spent about twenty minutes taking pictures. By the end of the session, the other girls had finally relaxed, too, even doing some silly poses. Sylvia glanced at the clock for the hundredth time. Still no sign of the photographer … or her mother, for that matter. It was getting late.

"I'm just going to try his number again." Sylvia picked up her cell phone. We all held our breath as she dialed and waited. Then we all exhaled with a sigh as she tossed it back onto the table with a growl of frustration. "And where is my mother?"

"I can answer that." Lizete held up her own cell phone. "Apparently she wasn't feeling well, so she's laying down in the air conditioning. My mom's with her, and she said she'll meet us at the Sunken Gardens in a bit."

"She's been in this hotel ... two doors down this whole time?" Sylvia stared at Lizete incredulously and then a small noise escaped her throat. I began to worry about her blood pressure. "This is difficult for her, I know, but she better not be creating drama on purpose."

Lizete shrugged and adjusted the ruffles on her strapless dress. "You know *sua mãe*. She said she'll support you today so she will. Maybe not without reminding you how she really feels, though."

They shared a knowing look.

"Hey, I know where Pete lives," Charlie said, stuffing her camera into a black bag. "His studio's in his house. It's not too far from here. I can drive over there and see if I can find out anything."

"That'd be great, Charlie. It's time for us to head down to the limo anyway." I picked up my bag and Sylvia's bouquet. "Everyone ready?"

Sylvia made the sign of the cross over her chest, forced a smile and nodded. Lizete squeezed her hand. "*Si*, let's go."

I pulled Charlie aside and whispered, "I'll keep my phone with me. Call as soon as you know anything."

"Will do."

I could tell Sylvia's cousins were trying to distract her from the current dilemma, chatting away in Portuguese and keeping her champagne glass filled from the bar inside the limo. But, I could also feel the waves of frustration floating around the small rectangular leather and glass space that we'd all been squashed into, along with a massive amount of dress material. It was there in Sylvia's charcoal-lined, dark eyes every time they met mine.

By the time the limo pulled up in front of the Sunken Gardens, I was a bit nauseous from the combination of champagne on an empty stomach and the heightened emotions. Gratefully, I scooted out of the air-conditioned limo and breathed in the humid August air. The sun was bright and there were some mumblings about the heat from the other girls, but otherwise our arrival was uneventful.

I took Sylvia's hands in mine as her cousins fluffed out her dress train, smoothed down some stray hairs and straightened her pearl and crystal tiara.

"*Perfeito*," several of them said in unison.

"If that means perfect, I agree." I smiled at Sylvia. "All right. I'm going to go check the ceremony area. Maybe the photographer just got confused, and he's photographing the guy folk first. You okay?"

She sucked in a shuttering breath and forced a brave smile. "*Si*. Thank you, Darwin. I'm sure you're right."

I followed the bricked pathway down to the shaded area where some guests were already seated in the white folding chairs. Flowered tiki torches stood every third row and white tulle had been strung between them, creating the path Sylvia would take to the wooden, flower-adorned archway where Landon now stood—his German Shepherd, Mage, and three groomsmen at his side. There goes my theory that the photographer might've come here first.

The guests were chatting amongst themselves and the sing song of tropical birds mingled with their voices. A multitude of sweet garden smells drifted in on the slight breeze. If I didn't know something was wrong, I would've taken a moment to enjoy the peacefulness and beauty of it all.

My sisters, Mallory and Willow, were seated in the second row. They'd arrived last night from Savannah. Next to them sat Frankie, my eccentric millionaire friend. Just seeing them here brought down my anxiety levels a notch as they were all laughing about something. Willow must've spotted the worry on my face, though. She stood up to give me a hug as I approached. Her long brown hair held a spicy scent, like sandalwood, and I leaned into her grounding energy.

"What's happened?" she asked.

I shifted my weight, trying to relieve the pain in my toes from the unfamiliar shoes I had on. "The photographer never showed up at the Vinoy. We were hoping he was here."

Frankie was fanning herself with an eggplant-colored satin clutch that matched her sleeveless, eggplant-colored dress and completely clashed with her bright red hair. Somehow this worked for her, though, making her appear fashion-brave instead of fashion-challenged. Being the eternal optimist, she said, "I haven't seen him, but I'm sure he's on his way, sugarplum."

Willow and Mallory shared a silent glance.

"Stop that," I whispered, knowing that look meant they sensed impending disaster. "Everything'll be fine."

"Whatever you say, Sis." Mallory's green eyes glowed as she smiled up at me smugly. Her long, auburn hair was pulled back in a French braid and the smattering of freckles across her nose were more visible in the sunlight. She was the baby at eighteen and still found life's sticky spots entertaining. Especially when I was involved.

"I'm sure it will." Willow shot her a chastising look. "Let us know if we can do anything."

"Thanks." I glanced around and was surprised to see Sylvia's mother seated in the front row. "Oh, how long has Mrs. Alvarez been here?" I asked.

Willow followed my gaze. "She arrived right before you did. She doesn't look very happy, does she?"

"No, she doesn't." In fact, she looked pale and worried. Another elderly, petite woman was talking to her and patting her hand. The fact that she was wearing a black blazer and skirt more suited for a funeral did not go unnoticed. Not the way you want your mother to look on your wedding day. I should go let her know Sylvia and the girls are here. "I'll be right back."

"Mrs. Alvarez, how are you?"

She lifted her chin and stared at me with round dark eyes and a downturned mouth. "*Eu sou quente.*" She waved a hand clutching a Kleenex. "Is hot, no?"

I smiled politely. "Yes, but at least we have some shade here in the garden."

"Getting married in garden," Ms. Alvarez scowled as she wiped her upper lip with the Kleenex. "Sylvia, she should be getting married in a church, where there is God and air conditioning."

Oh heavens, how did I manage to give her an opening for that comment already? "Well, I just wanted to let you know Sylvia and the girls are here."

Luckily, Will chose that moment to leave his spot at Landon's side and save me.

"Don't you clean up nicely, Detective." I tried to stay positive as I greeted him with a quick hug, but I felt the same worry coming off of him. This was not looking good.

Landon was also in front of me within a couple of strides, his ever-loyal German Shepherd, Mage, at his heels. Despite the groom-to-be's crisp, polished appearance, anxiety pinched the edges of his mouth and dark eyes, and a sheen of sweat had formed above his freshly shaven lip.

"Darwin, the photographer was supposed to be here to do the photos with the groomsmen before the ceremony started. Is he finished with the girls yet?"

Nope, not good at all.

I placed a hand on his arm to brace him. "Actually, Landon, he never showed up at the Vinoy. We were kinda hoping he was here."

"What? He never showed up?"

I held up my hand, trying to stop the rush of anxiety I could see discoloring Landon's cheeks. "Don't panic yet. Charlie's on her way to his house right now to see if he's there. Maybe he's just having car trouble, and she can give him a ride back."

He pinched the bridge of his nose. Will placed a comforting hand on his shoulder.

My phone buzzed in my hand. "Ah! That's her now. Hey, Charlie, find out anything?"

"Uh, you'd better have Will come over here ..." Her voice sounded strained.

My calm façade crumbled, my gut clenching under my red satin bridesmaid's dress. "What? Why?"

"Pete's dead."

CHAPTER THREE

I thought Sylvia was going to faint when I broke the news to her.

In a surprising burst of speed with all those layers of cascading ruffles, she hoofed it down the path and rushed into view of the waiting guests—a white sequined and taffeta bird startled into flight.

I half-ran, half-hopped, cursing the torturous heels as I tried to keep up with her and then slowed, torn between staying to comfort her or going with Will to find out what had happened.

I made it to the ceremony area in time to hear the flurry of Portuguese as she relayed the news to her family. Haunting wails immediately erupted from her mother.

Landon moved quickly to comfort Sylvia. Voices rose and a crowd gathered around her. Her cousins hurried past me and joined in the wailing.

I decided she had enough support with her family there. Hiking up my dress to free my legs, I ran back to catch Will in the parking lot. Well, I tried to run, but twisted my ankle and went back to hopping.

When I caught Will at his car and fell into the passenger seat, panting and red-faced, his mouth twitched.

"You sure you don't want to stay here with Sylvia?" He loosened his bow tie and motioned back the way I had come. "A wedding is much more pleasant than where I'm going."

I buckled my seatbelt, trying to catch my breath. "You haven't seen Sylvia's family upset." I shook my head. "Besides, Charlie sounded really shaken up, and I feel like the worst friend in the world for letting her go there alone."

Will moved his hand to mine and squeezed. "All right. Let's go find out what happened then."

We pulled up alongside the yard of the Placido Way address Charlie had given me. The scream of sirens were getting closer. I jumped out of the car and winced as my twisted ankle failed to support me. Stifling a curse word, I limped down the red-bricked path. Charlie was waiting on the porch step of Peter Vanek's tan and brown ranch style home.

"Are you all right?" I hugged her. Her face was blotchy and tear stained.

"Better than Pete." She jerked a thumb toward the cracked open front door behind her.

Will approached, carrying protective gear in a plastic bag under his arm and a notebook in his hand. "Charlie, I need you to start from the beginning and tell me exactly what happened when you got here."

She nodded and sniffed. "I went to knock on the door, but saw it was ajar. So, I pushed it wider and yelled for Pete. After a few seconds, I could hear a dog barking, but he didn't come to the door. So, I yelled again, louder. Something just didn't feel right. The lights were all on, but it was too quiet. I stepped into the house and there he was, a little further on down the hallway across from the kitchen ... just ... just lying there with his eyes wide opened." She shuddered, her fists gripping the edges of her blue cotton dress. "I checked for a pulse but he was obviously gone. That's when I ran out and called you, Darwin."

"All right. Thank you. You girls stay here."

No problem. Seeing a dead body was not on my to-do list today.

Will trudged up the wide, brick steps onto the porch. We watched as he tore open the plastic bag and dressed himself in the protective gear, including slipping paper booties over his shoes. He then pushed the door open wider with a gloved hand and disappeared through it.

"Why'd he do that? Put on all that stuff?" Charlie asked. "Is he treating this as a crime scene?"

"Don't worry. They have to treat every death as a possible crime."

The puppy's faint, desperate yipping reached us through the wide-open door. Poor thing. It must be confined or surely it'd be running out here to greet us.

Maybe the puppy saw something? I'd have to hold it and see if I could get any images from it. But for now, my attention stayed on Charlie. I slid an arm around her. Her skin was hot and flushed. The tiny diamond in her nose-piercing glittered in the sunlight. She stared at the grass in obvious shock.

"I'm sorry you had to find Peter like that. I can't even imagine how awful that must've been. Were there any signs of trauma?"

She rested her head on my shoulder. "No, none that I could see. He actually looked sort of peaceful. Except for his eyes being wide open, which was beyond creepy. He could've been sleeping. He's all dressed up, wearing a black tux, shoes and everything like he was getting ready to leave for the wedding when he ... he must've just collapsed."

A patrol car pulled up behind Will's sedan, its lights whirling, and right behind it came an ambulance, firetruck and a second unmarked sedan. I recognized the two officers who'd exited the patrol car and were now making their way down the brick path toward us with the ambulance crew close behind.

I raised my hand in greeting when they arrived. "Hey, y'all. Will's inside."

"Thanks, Darwin." Officer Fisch turned to the ambulance crew behind them. "You two wait here. I'll let Detective Blake know you're here and have you sign in." He looked back at us. "You girls doin' all right?"

"Hangin' in there," I answered.

He nodded and turned to his partner, handing him a roll of yellow crime scene tape. "You go on and get this place cordoned off." He glanced around the area. "I guess make the perimeter the entire yard and driveway to be safe." He tapped the clipboard in his left hand. "I'll take care of the security log."

Once again, my attention was drawn to the puppy, who's barking had turned to desperate whining. If there was no obvious cause of death, I might be able to help. I needed to hold the puppy. Luckily, Will reappeared at that moment.

I waited until he finished talking with Officer Fisch and the ambulance crew, then stood and motioned him over.

He had his mask pulled down beneath his chin, and he looked hot and frustrated. "What's up?"

"I can hear the dog inside." I raised an eyebrow. "Can you let me hold him?"

Will started to speak and then caught himself. I saw it hit him ... the understanding of exactly what I was asking and what it meant, the uncertainty, the battle and then the moment he gave in with a frown. "Sure. Wait here."

He returned carrying a soft travel crate. I ignored the fact he wouldn't make eye contact with me as he handed the crate over. Instead, I lifted the crate and peered inside. Two glistening black eyes and a pink tongue greeted me from the shadows. I smiled. "Well, hello there, cutie pie." I glanced back up at Will. "It's a Yorkie pup. I'm just gonna take him out in the yard."

"Yeah, sure. Let me know if ... you know." He mumbled something else, nodded and then disappeared again.

"I will," I said to the empty air. Well, at least he believed in my connection with animals now. He would get comfortable with it eventually, right?

I'd kicked my shoes off and squatted above the grass as I unzipped the carrier. I didn't feel like getting grass stains on a five hundred dollar bridesmaid's dress, even if the chances of me ever wearing it again were slim.

"Come on out, cutie pie. Come on, we're not gonna hurt ya," I coaxed, making soft kissy sounds.

The pup stuck a tiny black nose out of the bag opening, sniffed the grass and then pounced on it with zeal. I laughed as he rolled around, a brown and black fluff ball showing us his little pink, freckled belly. He jumped up and nipped at the hem of my dress and then took off through the thick grass. He was surprisingly quick for a creature with two inch legs.

"I'll get him." Charlie pushed herself off of the step.

I watched her catch up to him only when he stopped to pee. She scooped him up when he was finished and held him to her. "Stop that!" she cried as he bit her earlobe. "He's got baby vampire teeth," she squealed, handing him over to me. But she was smiling, which was nice to see.

As I wrapped my fingers around his tiny body, a current of energy zinged up my spine and then branched out through my arms and legs. An image flashed in my mind—a woman's elegant hand with French manicured nails. A giant diamond engagement ring with rubies and sapphires on either side. A feeling of confusion washed over me. A flash of hardwood floor through black mesh. A burst of frustration the color of red light.

The pressure built inside my head until a small "pop!" in my ears signaled its release.

I sighed. Well, that wasn't a very strong vision, more like an echo of the event. I held the puppy close and let him furiously kiss my chin, then I wiped at the tear stains on either side of his nose with my thumb before squatting and putting him back in the carrier. "Poor little thing."

That was disappointing. Not the high intensity trauma one would expect from a puppy if he'd witnessed his owner's death. I bit the inside of my lip and watched the Medical Examiner's van pull up as I thought about that gorgeous ring and wondered who owned it. Guess it didn't matter anyway. The vision probably had nothing to do with what had happened here this morning.

We watched as the M.E. and two crime scene techs exited the van and proceeded to slip into white suits similar to what Will had put on. We moved out of their way as they carried their equipment up the step and into the house.

While we waited, I played with the leather tag hanging from the carrier. It seemed like Peter Vanek was getting ready to take this puppy somewhere. Maybe to someone who'd watch it while he photographed Sylvia's wedding?

I glanced over at Charlie, who obviously had no qualms about grass stains as she'd opted to sit in the yard beside the porch. "This isn't Peter's name on here. It's a woman's. His girlfriend, maybe?"

She shrugged. "He never mentioned a girlfriend, but I didn't know much about his personal life. Only that he was passionate about helping unwanted animals. That's mostly what we talked about. Ways to help stray and abused animals, and photography, of course." She plucked at the grass.

"He really hated the whole shelter situation. That's why he tried to train as many willing students as he can … could … to take photos of the dogs dressed up in cute outfits. He said it really made a difference in finding them homes. Helped humanize them." She smiled sadly. "He had this big dream, you know. He talked about it all the time. He wanted to build a no-kill shelter on enough land so the animals weren't stuck living out their lives in small cages while waiting for their forever homes." She sniffed and wiped at her nose with the back of her hand. "He was one of the most kind-hearted people I've ever met. I can't believe he's gone. It's so surreal."

"I'm truly sorry. His death seems like a terrible loss ... for people and for the animals."

We sat silently for a little while after that. Resting my head against the porch railing, I closed my eyes and reached out with my mind to the water behind the house. The tension melted from my body almost immediately and, as my chest relaxed, my breath came easier.

Being half water elemental sure came in handy at times like this. As much as I complained about being a freak, I didn't appreciate the stress relieving part of it near enough. Waiting to find out what had happened to Peter Vanek was torturous, especially with the tiny gnats dive bombing our eyes and nose.

"Good God, these things are annoying," Charlie said, swiping at her face. She stood and dusted off her hands. "I've gotta do something. I'm going crazy."

I unzipped the travel carrier. "Here, play with this little ball of love for a bit."

I watched her for about fifteen minutes, chasing the puppy in the grass, then letting it chase her. He rolled around, chased his own tail, took a tumble dashing after a dragonfly, and barked and leaped at nothing until he was just plumb tuckered out.

Charlie carried the Yorkie back over. It was panting and both of them looked more relaxed. She sat back down with the pup in her lap. It only took a few seconds for him to fall asleep.

"When he's done with his little cat nap, we're going to have to get him some water," Charlie said.

Nodding in agreement, I reached over and stroked between his ears with an index finger. "Also, if this is Peter's girlfriend's puppy, we probably need to get it back to her and give her the bad news."

After another long stretch of time, Will finally stepped back out on the porch and removed his mask, hoodie and gloves. His gaze found mine. I pushed myself up and limped up the step to him.

"Are you all right?" He motioned to my ankle.

"Yeah, just twisted the darn thing. It'll be fine."

He nodded toward the puppy curled up in Charlie's lap. "Well, anything?" he asked warily. He didn't seem excited about the prospect of getting a clue this way.

I shook my head and detected a note of relief on his face. "Just an image of a lady's hand, wearing a huge engagement ring. And some crappy emotions with it. But, there's a name on the dog carrier. It's a woman's name and number. A Rachel Jennson. Should I call it and see if she's the dog's owner?"

"Is there an address?"

"Yeah."

"We'll just stop by then. If she knows him, I'd like to see her reaction to his death."

I crossed my arms and studied the tightness in his jawline. "Are you thinking foul play?"

Will shrugged noncommittally. "M.E. right now says it looks like a heart attack. We won't know for sure until the autopsy, but I couldn't find Mr. Vanek's camera anywhere. Surely, if he was about to leave for Sylvia's wedding, his camera would be packed up and ready to go, either in the house somewhere or already in his car."

I stared at the front door. "Charlie said he has a studio here at the house, did you check in there?"

"Yes. A quick sweep turned up some lenses and other gear, but no cameras."

"Huh. That is weird. So maybe a robbery gone wrong? He does seem a bit young for a heart attack."

"If he didn't have any pre-existing heart condition, yes he does. But why steal the cameras and not the lenses?"

CHAPTER FOUR

We sent Charlie back to The Sunken Gardens to give Sylvia the scoop on what we knew so far, while we drove the puppy to the address on the carrier.

"There, that's it. On the left." I pointed to a large beige, Spanish-style home sitting back from the road. Will pulled into the driveway, and I grabbed the carrier from the backseat.

Her landscaping was the usual variety of large and small palm trees, silver saw palmettos, a couple of overgrown bird-of-paradise, some pink dwarf oleander. I eyed that. It was pretty close to the sidewalk. I hoped she knew it was poisonous and kept this little guy away from it.

The doorbell made a soft chiming sound. After a few seconds, the door swung open and a young woman stood before us.

No, make that a goddess. A half-naked goddess at that.

She stood there in a red bikini that barely covered her curves, her skin a flawless caramel, her dark hair like silk falling over her shoulder, and her amber eyes glittering with curiosity.

She raised a perfectly shaped eyebrow as she raked Will with her gaze. "Yes? Can I help you?"

Something unfamiliar stirred in my chest like a bristling cat. Even her voice was inviting. Talk about winning the genetic lottery.

At that moment I realized I wasn't the only one mesmerized by her. The bristling cat tensed within me. I nudged Will with my elbow.

"Yes." He cleared his throat and kept his gaze purposely fixed on her eyes. "Are you Rachel Jensson?"

"Yes."

"I'm Detective Blake and this is Darwin. We've just come from Peter Vanek's home and this puppy was found there." He pointed at the carrier. "Your name and address are on the carrier. Is he yours?"

Leaning over, she peered in at the puppy, and I felt the carrier jiggle as the little guy shifted forward and yipped excitedly.

I also noted Will was suddenly interested in the wood frame above her head. What a gentleman.

Thankfully, she stood back up. "He was. I gave him to Petey last week to try and find him a home. I think Petey was getting attached to him, though." Her attention shifted from the puppy to Will. She looked him up and down, her eyes narrowing. "Do all detectives wear tuxes to make house calls?"

"We're supposed to be at a friend's wedding. Mr. Vanek was the photographer hired to shoot the wedding, but he didn't show up."

A fleeting cloud of worry passed over her expression. Mostly her eyes, the rest of her face didn't move much. Maybe genetics weren't solely responsible for her perfection after all.

She crossed her arms. "Well, that's not like him at all. Did something happen? Is that why you're here?"

"May we come in?"

"Yes. Of course." She stepped aside to let us enter and a knot formed in my stomach as I caught a whiff of her perfume. She even smelled good.

Stop it, Darwin.

What in blue blazes was wrong with me? Why did it bother me that this gorgeous woman also smelled nice? Did I really need her to be flawed in some way?

She led us through the entranceway to an open living room, which was littered with clothes, shoes and empty water bottles. She moved a pile of dresses off the cream sofa. "Please sit."

The puppy began to yip even more and scratch at the carrier door.

"Do you mind if I let him out?" I asked.

She nodded at me as she plopped down on the loveseat across from us and crossed her long, toned legs. Then she turned her concerned gaze to Will, biting her lip. "You look like you have bad news."

I hesitated, still trying to figure out if her nod meant, 'Yes, go ahead and let him out' or 'Yes, I mind if you let him out.'

"I'm afraid I do." Will tugged on his tux jacket. He seemed uncomfortable.

I frowned. That was new. He always seemed so confident and at ease.

Will cleared his throat. "Peter Vanek was discovered in his home a bit ago ... deceased."

We both watched her carefully.

She stared at us for a moment and then shook her head, her eyes darting back and forth between us while her expression stayed frozen. "What do you mean, deceased? Like, dead?"

"Yes."

"What? How?" Her complexion had paled, the glow she'd had before now morphed into pink blotches.

I was trying not to be secretly happy. Maybe she was an ugly crier. A sound by my foot startled me. The water inside one of the discarded water bottles sloshed around. *Oops!* I glanced at Will but he wasn't paying attention, thank heavens.

Mortified at the thoughts running amok in my head, I pushed them aside. Not to mention the loss of control of my water magick. Unacceptable. I'd have to examine where this darkness was coming from later, because I didn't like it one bit. It made me feel sticky and dirty inside.

Will was saying, "There was no obvious trauma. It looks like a heart attack, but we won't know for sure until the autopsy. Miss Jennson, how well did you know Peter Vanek?"

The puppy was scratching furiously now and had started a low, frustrated growl. I decided it was better to let him out so he wouldn't be such a distraction. I unzipped the carrier.

Rachel Jennson dabbed at the tears that were now falling like drops of crystals rolling off her waterproof face. Not an ugly crier then.

"Pretty well. I've worked with him for five years so we'd become good friends. He always said I was his muse. Most of my modeling portfolio is his work." A soft sigh punctuated her words. "I can't believe he's … gone. Who am I going to trust with my career now?"

The puppy hopped from the carrier, crossed the room and began scratching at her legs and whining.

She scooped him up absentmindedly with one hand and settled him on her lap.

I checked her hands, no engagement ring. So, it wasn't her hand in the vision. Unless she didn't wear the ring all the time. It was pretty big. Either way, the puppy must have gotten attached to her before she gave him to Peter. It also didn't escape my attention how elegant her perfectly manicured French nails made her hands. I hid my bitten nails under my legs and forced my thoughts back on track.

Why did she get a puppy if she didn't want one?

Will had leaned forward. "Did Mr. Vanek have any medical conditions that you were aware of?"

She shook her head and flicked her long hair over one shoulder. "No. He was a health nut actually. A vegetarian, very active. In fact, we often worked out together."

Yeah, I bet you did. I mentally smacked myself.

But Will must've had the same thought because he asked, "So, your relationship wasn't purely... professional?"

"Like I said, we'd become friends over years of working together. But, nothing romantic if that's what you're asking. He wasn't my type. Too short on both looks and money."

At least she was honest.

"Did he have any personal problems? Girlfriend? Enemies?"

"Well, my boyfriend, C.J., didn't like him. He was jealous of all the time we spent together. I tried to explain to him how important it is for a model and photographer to have a partnership, not just a business arrangement. The rapport is essential. We had to be comfortable around each other. I had to trust him to shoot me in the nude, to see me as a work of art and not a naked woman. You know, classy stuff, not porn."

She rolled her eyes. "Of course, C.J. says no man can look at a naked woman and not see a naked woman. He tried to get past it. He'd been doing better controlling his jealous streak, but he really flipped when I gave Petey this little guy." She motioned to the puppy curled up against her flat stomach and stroked his head with one knuckle. "It was C.J. who gave him to me." She glanced up. "But, anyway, he wouldn't have killed Petey over it, if that's what you're asking."

I glanced over at Will and frowned. He seemed to be studying the dog intently. Or was it the toned body the pup was curled up against?

Pushing aside these new disturbing thoughts and emotions with effort, I cleared my throat. "Ms. Jennson, the puppy seems really attached to you. Why did you give him to Peter to find a new home?"

Glancing down, she sighed softly. "Don't get me wrong, he's a cute little guy. And the photo shoot we did with him came out amazing. But I travel so much, I just can't have a pet. I mean, I hadn't even had time to think of a name for him. I leave for Paris in a week, and I'll be traveling for two months."

She shook her head. "It wasn't really a smart gift for C.J. to give me. I think he was trying to appeal to my maternal side, honestly. He's been bugging me lately about settling down and marrying him. Maybe when I'm too old to model anymore, like thirty. But right now, I'm at the top of my game, making a ton of money, traveling the world, in control of my own life. No man is worth giving that up for."

She threw a conspiratorial glance my way, but I couldn't relate to making "a ton of money" off of my body, so I just forced a polite smile.

Will was tapping his foot. "Was there anyone else, besides your boyfriend, who might've had a problem with Mr. Vanek?"

She thought for a moment then shrugged. "His neighbor's suing him. Petey was pretty upset about it, said it would ruin him financially if he lost. Something about damage to the neighbor's boat. The guy is a real creep, though. Always ended up in the yard when I was there, watering his plants in just his shorts. Like he really waters his own plants. Give me a break."

"Do you have a name for this neighbor?"

"Petey just called him the Jerry the Jerk."

"Okay, thank you." Will scribbled in his notebook. "We'll talk to him. Also, I'd like to speak with your boyfriend, C.J., and anyone else that was an acquaint-tance of Mr. Vanek."

I glanced at Will. I was really surprised he was going this far in the investigation already. I mean, what if the poor guy did just have a heart attack? Then I remembered the missing camera. It didn't just get up and walk out of the house by itself. Something was fishy.

"Sure. I'm actually having a party Monday night. Sort of a going away party. You should come. C.J. will be here and a lot of the other models Petey worked with and other industry people he hung out with. It's here at six."

Will nodded. "I'll stop by. Thank you."

"Actually, *we*'ll stop by, if you don't mind," I blurted out. No way Will was going to a party full of models without me.

"Oh." She flicked her gaze from Will to me and shrugged a sculpted shoulder. "Sure. It's casual dress."

I felt Will's curious glance aimed at me. Then he stood up. "I guess we'll see you Monday night. Thank you for your time."

"Such a shame." She rose and walked over, the puppy clutched to her chest. Then she placed her well-manicured hand on Will's arm.

I fought a growl.

"You'll let me know if you find out anything before then, won't you, Detective?"

"If I can."

"Thank you." She gave the puppy a kiss on the nose and maneuvered him back in the carrier. "You be good now, so these nice folks can find you a home."

I glanced at Will waiting for him to tell her it shouldn't be our job to find the puppy a home. But he didn't. He just shook her hand, thanked her again and we left.

Guess it was our job now.

CHAPTER FIVE

"What do you think?" I buckled my seat belt and slipped off the high-heeled red sandals Sylvia had ordered to match our dresses. I'd had enough of them and my ankle was throbbing. "Do you think she was telling the truth?"

"She seemed sincere."

I eyed Will's profile. He was chewing the inside of his cheek and seemed distracted. Which, I guess would be normal in the middle of a death investigation, but I couldn't help but wonder if he was more distracted by the bikini.

"She was real pretty," I ventured, still staring at him.

"Yeah." He signaled and changed lanes. As he did, he caught my stare.

Was I squinting? I made an effort to smooth out my expression.

"What?" he asked.

"So, you think she was pretty?" What was I doing? Of course she was pretty. Beyond just pretty, she was perfect. What was he supposed to say? I wanted to take the question/accusation back, but there was some new force controlling my mouth. One I didn't like at all.

"Yes, she was pretty. She's a model, sort of a job requirement." He laughed and then glanced back at me. "Wait a minute … are you jealous?"

I felt my face heat up. "No, of course not. Who would be jealous of her?" Tears pricked my eyes. I blinked in surprise. What in heaven's name was wrong with my body? Sanity had left the building.

Will rested his hand on my knee. "Darwin, you have to know I'm not that shallow. To me, you're the most beautiful girl in the universe."

I sniffed and smiled despite knowing he was lying to make me feel better. "Liar. You don't even know all the girls in the universe."

"Doesn't matter. Besides your outer beauty, you have an inner beauty, kindness and light that is very unique. You're a special person and I'm glad you're mine."

"Oh I'm yours, am I?" I joked, trying to lighten the mood.

A deep chuckle rumbled in his throat as he squeezed my knee. "Yes, ma'am."

It worked, until I suddenly got an image of me and Zachary Faraday on the dream beach.

Whoa.

Against my will, the first night Zach had invaded my dreams played out all over again in my head.

The air shimmered around me like a desert mirage. Sugary sand warmed my bare feet, water circled me. Large white caps rose beyond the sandy shore, moving toward me and crashing at my feet. They lulled me, and I felt my body swaying as if responding to some beat I couldn't hear. What I could hear, over and above the crashing sea, was a rumbling. I could also feel it beneath the sand. I squinted through the gauzy air toward the looming mountain, gaining more detail as I stared. Like a sudden fireworks display, fluorescent red spewed from the mountain, igniting the air.

I took a few steps back and stumbled, landing with a soft thunk in the sand. A figure began to shimmer and solidify in front of me. I gasped. Zach.

He reached down and held out his hand. I stared into the depths of his dark eyes as I placed my hand in his, feeling the familiar sensation of heat spread through my body. He pulled me up to stand before him, releasing my hand but instead of letting me go, he slid it to my waist and pulled me closer. My hand went to his bare chest and laid there. A soft gasp escaped my lips. I glanced down at the tattoo on his chest and felt the sudden need to trace it. As my finger moved around the symbols, down toward where his pants hung low on his waist, he moaned. The symbols changed from black to fluorescent red. The same color as the lava shooting through the air behind us.

"Darwin." He whispered my name and it echoed all around us. His index finger tilted my chin up to meet his eyes once again. His mouth came down softly to touch mine. Heat spread to my core as he deepened the kiss. Lost. I was lost in him. Lost to him. His arm tightened around me, pressing me against his chest until I felt nothing but pressure, heat and passion. His grip, his kiss, his dark, hungry eyes clearly said "mine."

I tore my mouth from his with effort that almost made me black out. "No." I breathed. I watched his glistening lips turn up in a half smile.

He nodded. "In time."

I forced myself back to the present and rested my heated forehead against the cool window. Why did my thoughts want to derail me at every turn today?

The puppy's scratching caught my attention. I glanced into the backseat, glad for the distraction. "Well, I guess I'm fostering this little guy until I can find him a new home. Can we run by Peter's house so I can grab his food and whatever else he needs?"

"Sure. I need to check on the progress at the scene anyway and have a word with the neighbor."

My phone vibrated in the console. I picked it up. "Sylvia! You all right, hon?"

"Darwin, I'm so sorry. This is such a disaster. Don't bother coming back to the gardens, the wedding is off."

Off? Wait, what? "You mean postponed right?"

"No. I told you this would happen. My mother believes the photographer having a heart attack is *um sinal de Deus.* God's way of telling us that the wedding is a mistake. I cannot have a wedding without my mother's support. To start a life with someone that way. It would never work out."

I pressed my palm against my forehead and closed my eyes.

Think, Darwin. Think. Should I try to talk Sylvia into getting married without her mother's blessing? No, Sylvia has a point. Her mother's disapproval might cause resentment and eventually drive a wedge between Sylvia and Landon.

My eyes popped open. "Okay, listen, Sylvia. Your mother believes the photographer's death was God's will, right? Because Peter died from natural causes?"

"*Si.*" She blew her nose.

"Well, what if he was actually murdered? An act of evil. Wouldn't that be the Devil trying to sabotage your happiness?"

She sniffed and then was silent for a moment. "*Si*, Maybe. But was he murdered? Who would want to kill my wedding photographer?"

"It's a possibility, and I don't know who or why. We just need a few days to prove it." I caught Will shaking his head out of the corner of my eye. I ignored him. "Here's what you need to do. Ask Frankie if she can get the Vinoy to extend your family's rooms for a week. She's got connections. Convince them they need to stay. Just a week. Tell them why and we'll get to the bottom of this for you, and then you can have the wedding with your mother's blessing."

Sylvia groaned and mumbled something I couldn't understand. "I don't know, Darwin. My mother, she's pretty stubborn when she makes her mind up about something. And the Sunken Gardens are booked up months in advance. I can't just change the date."

"But if the real cause of death is not natural, this'll change her mind and we can have the wedding, right? I mean, you can get married anywhere, it doesn't have to be at the Gardens."

Sylvia sighed. "*Si*. I think that would work. I can talk them into staying for a week if they can keep their rooms. But, how are you going to prove this one way or the other in a week?"

"You leave that part up to me and Will."

When I hung up, I glanced over at Will. He was smirking and shaking his head.

"What?"

"You know what you just promised her is impossible."

I adjusted myself in the seat so I was facing him, and gave him my most imploring puppy dog eyes. "Impossible? Where's your faith, Will? We have to do this. We have to prove that someone killed Peter Vanek in a week or the wedding is off for good. Sylvia and Landon's future depends on us."

"Us? Darwin, look, I know you want to fix this for them. But, I'm in the middle of helping Vice set up a huge drug sting involving one of my arson suspects. And even if I had nothing else on my plate, I can't just solve a murder in a week." He pulled up to a red light and turned to me. His shoulders fell when our eyes met, then he rested a hand on my knee. "You know I'd do anything for Sylvia and Landon. Anything within my power. But, a week? An investigation just doesn't work that fast even if I wanted it to." The light turned green and he sighed as he pressed the gas pedal. "Besides, we don't even know that Mr. Vanek didn't just have a heart attack."

I crossed my arms, my frustration and worry mounting. "I know you don't think he just had a heart attack or you wouldn't be starting your investigation already. We have to try. Please?" He shook his head slightly. I could tell he was thinking about it. "Please, Will."

He sighed and mumbled something as we pulled up to Peter's house. "Fine. We'll try. I'll see if I can get the autopsy pushed up. No promises."

Feeling a mixture of relief, gratitude and worry, I leaned over and pressed a kiss on his cheek. "Trying is all I ask."

CHAPTER SIX

Luckily for me, Peter's body had already been removed by the time we got back to his house.

While Will spoke with the officers who were just wrapping up, I let the puppy out of the carrier to go potty. He seemed more interested in rolling in the grass and chasing a tiny green dragonfly. I had to smile. He was a cute little thing.

After hopping after him on my sore ankle, I put him back in the carrier so I could gather his things from the house, including hopefully a harness and leash. If not, I'd have to stop by the pet boutique that Sylvia and I co-owned and grab one.

I kept my dog's food in the kitchen, so I tried there first. The kitchen was beautiful. It had black and gray marble countertops, shiny kitchen toys like a juicer, food processor, even a wheat-grass press. Proof that Rachel wasn't lying when she said he was a health nut. I felt more secure in my belief that this guy didn't have a heart attack.

I opened the pantry. Bingo. A bag of dried food and a stack of wet food cans. I didn't want to change his food and upset his stomach. Finding a couple of cloth grocery bags, I loaded them full of the dog food. What else? Peter probably also had a bed for him. I wandered down the hallway and found the master bedroom. Sure enough, there was a small round dog bed next to the dresser. I tucked it under my arm and then noticed a small basket of toys. I grabbed that, too.

A wave of sadness washed over me as I eyed the unmade bed, the photos on the dresser, the towel draped over a chair. All signs of a life that wouldn't continue. A life cut short.

One of the photos on the dresser was of a smiling Rachel with her arm draped over Peter. He was squinting into the sun, also smiling. Another photo was of him with a thin, elegant red-head. A wad of cash lay in a large seashell and a small, saliva-hardened stuffed bear sat next to the cash. Obviously a favorite dog toy. I grabbed it and tossed it into the toy basket.

As I lugged all the puppy stuff back down the hall, I paused in the office doorway. Will was standing near the desk, his head down, lost deep in thought.

Setting the bags, toys and dog bed down, I entered the room. Photos of stunning models, women and men, and brides covered the walls. Peter was obviously proud of his work. It was quite good. "Neighbor wasn't home?"

Will had his hands on his hips and didn't look up when he spoke. "No. I left my card."

"Something else wrong?"

He nodded. "The officers said there didn't appear to be anything else out of place, besides the missing camera. There was even cash lying on the bedroom dresser that wasn't touched."

"Yeah, I noticed that." I eyed one of the photos of Peter with the same pretty redhead as the photo on his dresser. In this one she wore an emerald green gown, and he wore a tux. His eyes sparkled kindly beneath wavy brown hair. He seemed happy. "But?"

"But there's a laptop charger lying on the floor behind the chair." He pointed beside the desk. "It's plugged in but no laptop. Plus I just made a more thorough check of his studio and still came up empty. The bags in there contain some lenses, flashes and other assorted equipment but no cameras. I don't think it's just one camera that's missing."

"Nothing in his car? The trunk maybe?"

"Nope. This could be a robbery. But then why not take the cash? The other valuables?"

I glanced around the office. "Maybe somethin' spooked 'em? They got scared off? Didn't have time?"

"Maybe. But still, how did he die? A heart attack at the same time as a robbery? Pretty coincidental. Unless he did have a heart condition and the fear from being robbed triggered it."

Will searched through Peter's desk drawers, his trash can, and then picked up a rolled-up paper on his desk and unrolled it. Finding nothing of interest, he rubbed his forehead with a rubber-gloved hand, then dug the car keys out of his pocket. "All right. Maybe forensics will come up with something. Let's get the puppy's stuff into the car and get you home."

When we got back to the car, I checked my phone and found a missed call and several text messages from my sisters. Apparently they'd left the Sunken Gardens and were waiting for me back at my townhouse above Darwin's Pet Boutique. It wasn't actually *my* townhouse. I was renting the million dollar city home above our pet boutique from Sylvia, who'd purchased it as an investment with her grandfather's inheritance money. But it was starting to feel like home.

By the tone of my sisters' messages, they weren't really worried about me, they just wanted the scoop.

Where are you???? Why aren't you answering your phone? Did you see the dead body???How'd he die? What's up with Sylvia's mother??Is the wedding off? Call us!

I smiled. I wanted to be irritated, but I was too happy to have them here.

* * *

"Well, I suppose you should give him a name at least." Willow had changed out of her dress into shorts and a Save-the-Earth t-shirt and was stretched out on my sofa watching the Yorkie puppy jump on my golden retriever, Goldie.

Goldie was being very good natured about the sneak attacks from the puppy nipping at her ears and tail. She'd even rolled over, her tail swishing lazily on the wood floor, obviously enjoying herself. The puppy tried to pounce on her belly, but only made it halfway before sliding down her shiny coat and falling over. Dog toys were strewn around them. It was great entertainment after a harrowing day.

"I should. You're right. Otherwise, he's going to start answering to 'hey puppy.'" I adjusted the ice pack on my ankle.

Mallory had stopped strumming her guitar and was scowling at me. Her long auburn hair was pulled up in a high ponytail and her face was scrubbed clean, making her look younger than her eighteen years.

"What?" I asked with more irritation than I should have.

Lucky—Mallory's black cat—was also staring at me from her perch above her mistress's shoulder. Both sets of green eyes were locked on me. "Ice? Really?"

I averted my gaze. I knew what she was accusing me of. It still bothered both my sisters that I wanted to live as normal a life as possible, without resorting to using the gift of elemental magick our father had passed down to us. My gift was water magick, Mallory's was fire and Willow's was earth. They were both proficient in using their gifts now. Me, I was back in magick kindergarten.

It was my fault, though. I'd stopped practicing and, unlike riding a bike, it wasn't something you could just jump back into at the same point of proficiency.

I wasn't keen on jumping back in anyway. The last time I'd used it, I'd almost ruined my relationship with Will. He still couldn't talk about it. It was the elephant in the room with us.

He's not exactly the open-minded type, which I really don't hold against him. I mean, it's what makes him a great detective ... just the facts, ma'am and all that. So how could I engage in something I knew would only put up a bigger wall between us? It would feel like I was doing something on purpose to sabotage our relationship.

"Leave her alone, Mal," Willow said, being the peacemaker as usual. "She has a right to decide when and if she'll use her magick."

"Thank you." I fought the urge to stick my tongue out at Mallory. It was hard to be a grown up around my family sometimes. Time to change the subject. "Okay, y'all have to help me come up with a name for the puppy."

After a few minutes of contemplation, Willow said, "What about Peter Junior? You know, to honor the photographer who died."

I nodded. "I like that actually. Maybe Petey would be better, though. Suits him more." Sliding down onto the floor, I called, "Petey, come here boy." He came, but only because Goldie noticed me on the floor and trotted over with the puppy at her heels. I scratched the thick, pale yellow fur on Goldie's chest as she plopped down and leaned against me. "You're such a good girl, letting this little devil climb all over you."

I laughed as Petey managed to climb up on my lap and stretch his front legs up on my chest, trying to reach my face with his postage-stamp-sized tongue. Such exuberance packed in such a tiny body. "You like your new name?" I lifted him a little to let him get a lick of my chin. It was like giving him an A for effort.

Goldie eyed him sideways, her tongue hanging out of her mouth like silly putty, lending her an expression of amusement.

"Speaking of the devil," Mallory said, resting an arm on her guitar, "there was an awful lot of talk about him going on between Sylvia's family members before we left. What's up with that?"

I lifted Petey higher and buried my nose in his silky hair, gave him a kiss on the head and then placed him back on the floor. He leaped from my hands and jumped onto his worn stuffed bear with a baby growl. It did seem to be his favorite toy. I was glad I'd grabbed it.

"Well, Sylvia's mom believes that the photographer's death was a sign from God that the wedding shouldn't happen. Honestly, Sylvia told me her mom already had her feathers ruffled over them not gettin' married in church, so this may be just the excuse she's looking for to withdraw her support. Who knows. But, if we can prove that Peter Vanek was murdered, then at least Sylvia could reason with her mother that Peter's death was the work of the devil, not God." I sighed. "Sylvia won't marry Landon without her mother's blessing."

"I see. Beliefs can be so complicated." Willow said. "Well, what can we do to lend a hand?"

I smiled softly. I was suddenly exhausted and overwhelmed by a wave of gratitude. Willow may be four years my junior, but she really was my rock. "If it turns out that Peter was murdered, we have one week to prove it before Sylvia's family flies back to Portugal and the wedding is off for good."

"Oh, that's all?" Mallory rolled her eyes. Lucky hopped to the floor and, tail twitching, chirped at her. Mallory tugged at the scrunchie in her hair, letting it fall around her shoulders. Then she tossed the scrunchie across the room.

Lucky charged, pounced on it with a half-purr, half-growl and then carried it back to her.

I shook my head. "I swear that cat thinks she's a dog."

Lucky had snagged Petey's attention. He scrambled after her, trying to catch her before she leaped gracefully back up on the sofa. He was too slow and let out a sharp bark of frustration.

"And speak of the *other* devil," Mallory said, "you-know-who was at the wedding."

My stomach fluttered as I met her worried gaze. I did know who. Zachary Faraday. Part jinn, part man-who-haunts my dreams, and *all* dark and mysterious. I already knew he'd be there since I helped Sylvia write out the invitations, but I'd made it a point not to look for him in the crowd.

"Of course he was there, Mal. He's a friend of Landon's." I could hear the quiver in my own voice. Fear was not the only cause of that, and I hated myself for it. "Did he talk to you?"

"He sure did. Both of us." Mallory flicked her hair over her shoulder as she frowned and tossed the scrunchie again. "I introduced Mr. Creepy to Willow. Tell Darwin what he said."

Willow shot her an irritated look and then turned to me. "I was going to wait to tell you since you have enough to worry about right now. But, since it's out there ... after he shook my hand, his eyes did this weird sparking-fire thing and he said, 'Be careful. All of you.'"

I narrowed my own eyes. "Like a threat?"

Willow shook her head emphatically. "No. More like a warning."

Mallory picked up Lucky and draped her over one shoulder like a security blanket. "Mr. Creepy's the only danger I see around here."

I was surprised that Mallory still considered him a threat after he'd helped us in a life-and-death situation once already. If it wasn't for him and Mallory working together when we were locked in that airport office, we'd all be toast. Obviously, he didn't want us harmed.

Willow's lips were pursed and her brown eyes narrowed. "I don't know. We at least know to be cautious with Zach Faraday. I think it's the danger we don't see that we should be more concerned about."

"You're taking his warning seriously then?" Mallory scoffed.

I thought back to last Halloween at Landon's party. Zach was doing psychic readings for Landon's guests. Before I knew it was actually *him* doing the readings, I'd ended up in front of him, my hands in his. It was unnerving to say the least. He knew things he shouldn't have known. He knew about my father. And about the danger I was about to be in. And he knew that we would face that danger together, which turned out to be true.

"I think we should take him seriously. Just to be on the safe side."

They both looked at me, Willow with a nod of agreement and Mallory with a smirk.

Petey suddenly yipped and we all jumped.

After laughing at ourselves, I said, "All right, y'all. I'm takin' the dogs out one last time and then I'm going to bed. We have an investigation to start tomorrow."

CHAPTER SEVEN

Between fighting off dreams of Zach and the puppy whining off and on all night, I felt like a zombie Sunday morning. I'd have to get some Aspen and Cherry Plum flower essence from the store today to comfort Petey. I wasn't sure what to do about Zach intruding into my dreams. Ignoring the situation wasn't working. I'd have to confront him at some point … just not today.

When I came downstairs with a squirming Petey tucked under my arm and Goldie at my heels, Willow was already up and busy in the kitchen.

"Good morning," she said, without turning her attention away from the stove. Lucky came over and wound herself around my feet, her motorboat purr going strong.

"I guess," I mumbled, not in the best mood. "Whatever that is, it smells delicious." I reached down and stroked Lucky's shiny black fur with my free hand. She happily arched her back into my palm.

"Grandma Winters' pumpkin pancakes. I noticed you have a slight canned pumpkin addiction." She grinned back at me.

"For the dog treats I make." I slipped into my flip flops and grabbed two leashes and a treat out of the jar on the counter. "Taking the dogs out. Be back."

The morning air was already sticky and warm, the sun beaming intensely at the world. Traffic was almost non-existent as I led the dogs across Beach Drive and into North Straub Park. This was very different from snowbird season when St. Pete would've already been packed with excited tourists ready to explore, eat and shop.

North Straub Park had quickly become my favorite place in the world. Well, my favorite place in the very small amount of places I'd ever been but still, there's a good reason. It was a sprawling, grassy area between the strip of shops and eateries on Beach Drive and the sparkling blue waters of the yacht basin. A huge banyan tree offered park-goers respite from the heat. The iconic Vinoy Renaissance Resort bordered the park on the north, the Fine Arts Museum on the south. A great place to start any day.

I sat Petey down in the grass as Goldie sniffed around. He froze for a second and then with a yip he hopped at Goldie, catching the tip of her tail in his teeth. She didn't even notice. Shaking my head I reached down and moved him away from her.

"Go potty."

It had occurred to me that even though he hadn't had an accident in the house yet, he may not be fully potty trained. He did seem pretty young. I watched him closely, cocking my head. He seemed to be squatting, though it was hard to tell with him only clearing the thick grass a few millimeters. When it appeared he'd peed, I said, "Good boy!" and fed him a piece of the homemade pumpkin treat I'd brought. Then we walked around a bit more, my thoughts going first to Sylvia's ruined wedding and then to Peter Vanek's ruined life. What a mess.

I consciously reached out to the Bay water to calm my nerves. I had to stay focused if I was going to be any help proving Peter didn't die from natural causes and saving my friend's wedding. Poor Landon. I couldn't even imagine what he was going through. He was supposed to be married to the woman he loved right now and on their honeymoon—

My thoughts were interrupted by a tingling sensation and the hair on my arms rising. I glanced around. Was someone watching me?

A couple with a black lab strolled along the water's edge and a lone woman sat beneath the big banyan tree, engrossed in a novel. Other than that, the park was empty.

Something didn't feel right, though. The air had solidified, growing hotter and heavier. Stifling. My heartbeat quickened in response to the unseen threat. I was confused, but I'd learned early on not to ignore my sixth sense.

I scooped up Petey, pulled a piece of grass from his mouth and hurried back across the street with both dogs to the safety of the gated townhouse.

* * *

"What were you looking at?" Mallory asked around a mouthful of pancake as I finally sat down at the table with them. I hadn't been able to shake the uneasy feeling, even after being inside. I had seen nothing out of the ordinary from my balcony view of the park. But still ...

"I don't know. Nothing I guess." I squeezed some local organic honey onto a pumpkin pancake. "It's just that when I was out there with the dogs, it felt like I was being watched. Probably just being paranoid."

"It could've been Zach ... he does act like your personal protection," Mallory offered, obvious disapproval in her tone.

"Maybe." I shrugged. Though, I didn't think so. This definitely felt threatening. But, I was done thinking about it for now. "Anyway, what do y'all want to do today? Hit the beach? Go shopping? A museum?"

There really wasn't anything I could do as far as the investigation went until I heard back from Will and wasting Sunday while Darwin's Pet Boutique was closed would be a sin. Especially when it'd been such a long time since the three of us had been together.

When I'd left our Savannah, Georgia home last summer to open Darwin's Pet Boutique with Sylvia and start a new life here, it had taken a while for my sisters to forgive me. It was nice to have them back in my life. Now if I could just get our mother to forgive me, but that was a whole other ball of wax.

"I could use some beach time," Willow said.

"Then shopping," Mallory added. "And dinner out at a nice restaurant. I haven't been to a restaurant since I was here back in October."

"Sounds like a plan." I glanced under the table where Petey's warm body was stretched out against my bare foot. Goldie was under there, too, lying so her nose was almost touching him. She was really getting attached to him. "Though we'll have to make a few trips back here during the day to let the dogs out."

It had been a while since I'd had a puppy, but I was starting to remember how much work they were. I scratched his belly with a bare toe, smiling. He was cute as a button. Shouldn't be hard finding him a home. The hard part would be not getting attached to him myself.

After breakfast, the three of us piled into my brand new white VW convertible Beetle in the parking garage. I'd just learned how to drive recently—Willow had taught me when she was here a few months ago—and this was the very first car I'd ever owned. I still felt a little jolt of excitement when the engine came to life.

Usually Goldie was my sidekick, so it was strange not to have her with me. I'd left her at home, much to her disappointment. Though the heat and sun didn't hurt us, it was going to be a high of 93 degrees today, way too hot for a dog on the beach.

Mallory feigned being terrified of my driving as I pulled out onto Beach Drive, but I knew she was just teasing. Both sisters were grinning from ear to ear. Driving was actually a new concept to all of us, due to an extremely over-protective mother growing up.

For some reason, Grandma Winters had up and decided to teach Willow how to drive on her last visit to Savannah. It was strange. Grandma Winters had always visited us twice a year, staying for two weeks at a time. And she only ever concerned herself with helping us grow our elemental gifts. She'd never been the cookies and bedtime-story type of grandma, or the type to teach us anything about the world. I wasn't complaining, though. Knowing how to drive gave us all more freedom, something our mother had always frowned upon. Freedom to her equaled danger.

I couldn't wait to soak my bones in the salty Bay water. It was my happy place. So, as my sisters set up their towels, I headed for a swim.

The water was warm, like bath water, and the blazing sun set the surface on fire with silver sparkles. It called to me and I felt my power surge in response. Nothing made my heart sing more. I relaxed, feeling my body sink into it, letting it wash over my head. When my toes hit the bottom, I opened my eyes. *Home.* That's what it felt like. Coming home.

I kept still and let the sand settle back to the bottom where I'd disturbed it. The water cleared. Tiny waves came from me and I sent them in a lazy circle, speeding them up until a small cyclical tornado spun in front of me. It felt safe to practice here, beneath the surface, out of sight of the rest of the world. If no one can see, it didn't really happen, right?

As I dispersed the tiny tornado and prepared to send it spinning the other way, a shape caught my eye. A dark shadow that seemed to be heading straight for me like a torpedo. My heart skipped.

A shark? Surely not this close to shore. Plus it was moving too fast.

I backpedaled instinctively as it quickly closed in on me. Sand kicked up by my feet clouded the water. I strained to see through it. Something was there in a flash. A face in front of me. I screamed bubbles and threw up my arm, closing my eyes. When I felt nothing attack, I dared to open my eyes.

Nothing.

Spinning around, I searched the water. My lungs ached for air. A small fish swam by. Launching myself upwards, I breached the surface and took a huge breath, shaking.

What in heaven's name was that?

I scrambled out of the water on legs heavy with fear and hurried back to the safety of my sisters. I kept shooting glances behind me to make sure I wasn't being followed.

Willow turned toward me as I collapsed in the sand. "Darwin, what's wrong? You look white as a ghost."

Mallory pushed herself up on one elbow and watched me. She got powered up by the sunlight, so her eyes were an almost fluorescent green. "Did something happen?"

I nodded. It was all I could manage until my heart stopped racing enough for me to breathe and talk at the same time. "Something came at me. In the water."

After I'd tried to explain the short but terrifying experience, Mallory asked, "So, do you think it was like a vision?"

I shook my head. "No. It was too real." I squeezed my eyes shut and, despite not wanting to, I forced myself to relive the moments under water. "I ... there was long hair. A face. I..." I opened my eyes. "I think it was a woman. But that's not possible, right?"

"A woman who came out of nowhere and disappeared just as quickly? Doesn't seem possible," Willow said skeptically. She sifted the sand through her fingers. I knew she was comforting herself. "Are you sure it wasn't just a stingray or maybe a manatee?"

The more I focused, the more I was sure. It was definitely a woman and something felt familiar about her. I met Willow's gaze and held it. "No. I know I sound completely off my rocker, but it was definitely a woman."

She shaded her eyes, scanning the water. "Okay. I believe you. Maybe this has something to do with the threat Zach warned us about."

Startled, I glanced out at the water. Its surface was a calm, light blue beneath the cloudless sky. But what was below the surface? Could it really be hiding a threat? "I guess it's time I had a talk with him."

"Darwin," Willow said, touching my arm. I turned my attention to her. She had that serious mouth-pinched expression that I remembered well from growing up. "I know I said you had the right to decide if you'd use your magick or not, but if this threat isn't human, you have to be able to defend yourself. You have to practice. It's time."

My spirit deflated like a punctured balloon. She was right, of course. I would have to practice, even though embracing the world of magick would mean actively building the wall higher between me and Will. A moan escaped me. Why did life have to be so complicated?

Mallory scooted closer and wrapped her arm around my shoulder. I could smell the heat emanating from her skin. It chased away the cold chill the woman's ghostly attack had left me with. Dropping my head onto her shoulder, I glared at the water.

Whatever that was about, the assailant had accomplished one thing. She'd stripped away my sense of security by attacking me in the one place I'd always felt safe.

* * *

After running home to let the dogs out, I'd left Willow and Mallory to go shopping without me. It was time to see a jinn about a warning.

As I pulled my VW Beetle around the circle drive in front of the gray stucco buildings of Golf Gate Estates, I kept my thoughts focused on meeting up with my sisters later for dinner.

Happy thoughts, Darwin. Happy thoughts.

Otherwise, I was afraid I would chicken out of what I was about to do. Which was knock on the end unit door marked 457 where Zach Faraday now resided.

My hand was poised to knock when the door flew open and Zach stood before me, all tense muscle and eyes blazing.

"Darwin." His relief was palpable.

I felt that relief wash over me as a soft, silky wave. Despite myself, I was touched by his obvious concern.

"Please, come in. Are you all right?"

"Right as rain." I stepped into the overly air-conditioned room. It was like an icebox. "I'd hate to have your electric bill," I mumbled, rubbing my bare arms and taking in the room.

All his mother's things were still in place—the thick burgundy curtains with tassels adorning the windows; the gold chandelier and spun gold tapestry hanging on the forest green wall, the photos on the fireplace mantle. Even the crystal ball still sat on the coffee table, though Zach had told me he himself doesn't scry. I would've thought he'd turned this place into a bachelor pad by now.

As I took a seat on the cream velour sofa, I caught the scent of jasmine and memories flooded back.

His mother, Rose Faraday, had been a gypsy fortune teller. She'd been Lucky's original owner, which is how Mallory ended up with the cat. We'd solved Rose's murder together last year—me, Zach and Mallory—and Zach had played a big part in saving mine and Mallory's life in the end.

It looked like he still wasn't ready to let his mother go. Or maybe he just hadn't had time for a garage sale yet, what with all the time he spent stalking me.

"I didn't even get a chance to knock." I didn't mean it to, but it came out like an accusation. "Were you expecting me?"

He lowered himself next to me, angled his body in my direction and rested a thick, muscular arm on the back of the sofa. "I was just on my way out. I sensed you were in danger."

My eyes narrowed.

He could sense I was in danger? Were we that connected?

I fought the urge to scoot back away from him. His body held a palpable amount of heat and power, and it was making it hard for me to think straight. I didn't want to appear rude, though, especially since I was here to get information from him. I stayed where I was ... in the danger zone. "Do you know why I'm here?"

He held my gaze then let his attention fall to my mouth. "Having trouble sleeping?"

My heart kicked up in a flutter of betrayal. My cheeks burned. We'd talk about him invading my dreams later. I crossed my arms like a shield in front of me. "I'm here because of the warning you gave my sister, for us to be careful. What did you mean by that?"

His dark eyes met mine once again. They were a pool of exotic mystery, so easy to get lost in.

He took a deep breath and then mercifully moved his attention to his mother's crystal ball on the coffee table. He still wasn't looking at me when he asked, "How much do you know about your father?"

"My father?" Anxiety tightened a knot in my chest. "Not much. Just that he's imprisoned for breaking some kind of rule ... that magick and mortals aren't supposed to mix. That is if he's even still alive and our mother isn't just telling us some insane story to hide the fact that he's not ... you know ... alive." A lifetime of frustration on the subject made me open up to him without a second thought. "Mom won't tell us anything except how they fell in love when she was seventeen, and Father moved her to his family's mansion in Savannah after she got pregnant with me. Do you know more about him?" I tried to keep the hope out of my voice but I wasn't successful.

Zach tilted his head and then turned fully towards me. He enfolded my hand between his own large, warm ones. It was effortless and for some reason, I didn't mind even though I should have. He closed his eyes and I felt the light vibration begin.

It traveled up my arm and into my body, pulling me closer to him and away from the physical world, until I could feel our heartbeats sync, feel his deep inhales in my own chest, feel myself falling into him. My free hand reached out and rested on his chest. I felt myself doing it but was powerless to stop it. It was the only thing I wanted, the only thing I needed in the world at that moment. To feel his heartbeat beneath my palm. The beat than ran through both of us in sync making us one body. There was nothing but that bliss of connection. I lost track of time.

When my eyes finally fluttered open, they met Zach's. His held a touch of surprise but also raw passion so fierce it knocked me back into my own orbit. I jerked my hand away and his tattoo, which had been burning red beneath my touch, ceased to glow through his white t-shirt.

I ripped my other hand from his grip and scrambled up on shaking legs. "I have to go."

Tears pricked my eyes as I bumped into furniture in my quest to escape and then fumbled to unlock the door.

Oh heavens, just let me get out. Please.

"Darwin." Zach's voice came from directly behind me.

I refused to turn around. I couldn't. I didn't trust myself. "Please open the door," I whispered.

Heat radiated from his chest as he moved closer behind me. Tears blurred my vision. His hand appeared and turned the knob. Before he let go, he tried once more. "I have to tell you what I know. It's important."

I would do anything to learn about my father. Anything except betray Will. If I stayed any longer, that's exactly what I'd do. "Later," I whispered. "Let me go."

"As you wish." His hand withdrew from the lock. The heat withdrew from my back, leaving me with a sense of cold loss as I stepped back out into the balmy air of the real world.

CHAPTER EIGHT

Since Sylvia was technically on her honeymoon for the week—though probably actually curled up on the sofa watching chick flicks with her cousins and eating ice-cream for breakfast—Mallory had come in to help me out at Darwin's Pet Boutique.

The snowbirds had abandoned St. Pete in May when the humidity moved back in, but we still had enough local clientele to stay afloat. And of course, Monday morning didn't get its feet under it until Frankie Maslow, one of my best and most eccentric friends, showed up with a box of pastries and the morning paper.

"Good morning," Frankie said as I unlocked the door and let her and her two Chihuahuas, Itty and Bitty, into the boutique.

She gave me a hug with the arm that wasn't cradling a box of ... *what was that?* Cinnamon buns, from the mouth-watering scent drifting from the pink box, which Goldie was now sniffing with interest.

"How's our Sylvia? Have you heard from her?" Frankie asked with concern.

I shrugged. "She wouldn't answer her phone yesterday, but she did text me late last night and just said she's alive but doesn't feel like talking." I nudged

Goldie out of the way so Frankie could set the box down on our tea table by the front window.

"Morning, Frankie." Mallory appeared from the back grooming room with Petey cradled in her arms. She was wearing Sylvia's water-proof apron over her mint-green maxi dress, and her hair was pulled up in a messy bun atop her head. "I smell cinnamon buns."

"Yes you do. Oh, sweet puppies in heaven! Who in the world do you have there?" Frankie's two plump Chihuahuas, dressed in pink and blue t-shirts respectively, were at her heels as she held out her hands with a grin. "Let me see that baby!"

"This is Petey, all fresh and smelling much better." Mallory handed him over and smirked at me. "It was like bathing a hamster."

Frankie rubbed her nose against Petey's and then laughed as he tried to chew on hers. Itty and Bitty scratched at her leopard print leggings, not happy their mom was giving another member of their tribe attention. "Feisty little guy. Where'd he come from?" She bent down to let her dogs sniff Petey.

"Actually, he came from Peter Vanek's place," I said. "The puppy didn't have a name yet, so we named him Petey in remembrance."

"Ouch." She stood back up. "Poor little guy lost his daddy?"

I slid into a wicker chair, the cushion already warmed by the morning sun pouring through the window, and helped myself to a gooey cinnamon bun. "Peter wasn't planning on keeping him. He was trying to find him a home. I don't think it'll be too hard, but if you know anybody that'd be a good fit, send 'em my way."

She handed the squirming black and brown ball of fur back to Mallory and came over to join me at the tea table. Itty and Bitty settled in beneath her feet and Goldie sprawled out with a loud sigh, watching us with hopeful eyes for any sign we were willing to share a cinnamon bun.

"Sure will," Frankie said, pouring herself a cup of hot tea. "I still can't believe Sylvia's luck. For her photographer to have a heart attack right before her wedding." She shook her head. "Her mother was not a happy camper. Though I couldn't really understand what all the fuss was about since they weren't speaking English. I mean, couldn't Sylvia just've had her guests take cell phone pictures and get on with the wedding?"

I shook some Iron Goddess Oolong tea into my diffuser and sank it into the hot water in my cup. "Well, Sylvia called off the wedding because her mother thinks Peter's death was a sign from God they shouldn't get married. And that their marriage would be cursed if they went through with it. Sylvia won't get married without her mother's blessing."

"Yikes." Frankie shook her head. "Poor Sylvia … and Landon."

"I know. The thing is, though, Will doesn't think it was a heart attack. He suspects foul play since none of Peter's cameras were found at his house. They didn't just grow legs and walk out the door themselves, right? Someone had to have stolen them."

"Interesting." Frankie's penciled-on eyebrows rose beneath her freshly dyed red hair as she pulled a bite-sized piece of sticky heaven off a roll and popped it into her mouth.

Mallory was unlocking the door with one hand, cradling Petey with the other. "I'm gonna take him out one more time before I put him in the pen."

I nodded. "Thanks. Make sure you give him a treat as soon as he goes potty."

We'd made sort of a doggie play pen with gates for Petey behind the counter so we didn't have to leave him in the crate upstairs while we worked today. Willow had plans to spend the afternoon with Kimi and Jade, some friends she'd made when she'd visited me a few months ago.

I turned back to Frankie. "Anyway, if we can prove Peter was actually murdered, Sylvia and Landon could still get married. We just have to prove it by Sunday."

"Ah, now I understand why she asked me to get their rooms extended. You think Will can figure out what happened in a week?"

I wrapped my hands around my tea cup and nodded. "If anyone can, it's Will. And of course, I'll help him however I can. He's actually open to me helping, if you can believe it."

She eyed me skeptically as she chewed. Then after she swallowed, she pointed a ruby-ring-clad index finger at me. "You better not put yourself in danger again, Darwin. After all, you've got Goldie to think about now. She's already lost one momma."

We both glanced down at my golden retriever, who raised her head hopefully and panted at us with sparkling eyes.

Goldie had been a show dog. After her owner had been killed, I ended up adopting her. She had a scar now, so she couldn't show anymore, which was fine with me. But, Frankie was right. She didn't deserve to go through that again. I'd have to be careful.

Giving in, I broke a piece of my cinnamon bun off and tossed it to her. She had trained me well in the five months I'd had her. "That's all you get." I laughed as she licked her muzzle and sat up with ears tilted forward. "All done, moocher."

Frankie opened the paper with a sharp snap. "All right, let's see what other mischief happened over the weekend in this crazy town."

Sipping my tea, I watched out the window as Mallory made her way back across the street toward us with Petey. I glanced over at the clock as she came back in. About that time.

"You can just leave it unlocked, Mal."

Charlie walked in behind her. She looked more like herself in a gray newsboy hat turned backwards, a black halter top, which showed off her full sleeve of tattoos, and white skinny jeans.

"Oh, hey, Charlie. What are you doin' here?"

"Just thought I'd stop by and see if you need any help today. And see if there's any news about Pete?"

"That's sweet of you, but I think I'm good. Mallory's helping me out. And as far as Peter goes no news yet, but I can tell you Will's thinking it may not have been a heart attack. He's gonna try to get the autopsy pushed up."

Charlie stopped petting Goldie and stared at me. "Why does he think that?"

"Because all Peter's cameras were missing and there was no sign of a laptop either, just a charging cord."

"So like a robbery gone bad?"

Goldie nudged Charlie's hand with her nose for more pets. Charlie obliged.

I shrugged. "Possibly."

Charlie froze. "Oh God. The thief could've still been there when I got there. Maybe I interrupted him and he slipped out the back or something?"

"You'll drive yourself crazy thinkin' about what-if's," I said.

"Come over here and help yourself to a cinnamon bun, Charlie, there's plenty," Frankie said, a bit distracted. "Oh, this is a shame," she clucked and then read to us from the newspaper. "The director at St. Pete Helping Paws Rescue is being investigated for fraud. 'Volunteer staff at the shelter have alerted board members to discrepancies on state forms,'" she read, "'which are used to gain subsidies from the state for low-income pet owners who use their mobile spay and neuter service.'"

She shook her head and glanced at us over her black rhinestone reading glasses. "I hope there's no truth to the accusations. I've known the shelter director, Sassy White, for years. She's good people, done a lot for animals in this community."

Charlie frowned as she settled into a chair beside us. "You know, Peter said something strange to me a couple weeks ago when we were leading a few dogs outside to photograph them for the website. I didn't think anything of it at the time, but he was glaring at the mobile spay and neuter van. And then he said, 'She's right, I don't think that van has moved all week.' And when I asked him what he meant, he said, 'never mind.' I agree with you, though, Frankie. Sassy's good people."

"Wonder what that's all about?" I asked.

But no one had time to answer as our first customer of the day came in, her excited Great Dane pulling on his lead. I hurried to get him a treat.

Customers trickled in at a fairly steady pace all morning. When Will showed up at one o'clock, I decided to let Mallory handle the store and ran upstairs to make us a picnic lunch.

We sat under the banyan tree in the park with our spread of food and took turns throwing a tennis ball for Goldie. Petey gnawed on a dehydrated sweet potato chew beside us. Once in a while he'd bark and paw at it, and Goldie would run over to make sure it wasn't hurting him.

She'd make a good big sister, but I really didn't think I could give a second dog the attention he deserved after my sisters left. Especially a puppy.

I unwrapped my sandwich and eyed Will. "Go on, spill it. You look like you're dying to tell me something. Is it about the case?"

Will glanced up, his blue eyes glittering in the sunlight. Sweat had beaded up on his forehead. He nodded. "It is. The M.E. did me a favor and did an initial exam of the body this morning. He found a suspicious needle prick on the back of Mr. Vanek's neck."

I stopped chewing. "Oh my stars. So..." I had trouble swallowing past the lump in my throat. "So like he was drugged?"

"Drugged. Poisoned. That we don't know yet. The ME has a theory based on the initial examination, considering the condition of the body, but he's ordered an expedited drug test to be sure."

"That's fantastic!"

Will raised an eyebrow and his mouth twitched.

"Oh, no, I don't mean it's fantastic that someone may have drugged or poisoned him. That is actually awful. But for Sylvia and Landon ... it's better than a heart attack. It means they at least have a chance of getting married."

He rested a warm hand on my bare calf. That warmth flowed straight to my heart. "I know what you meant. I've also sent officers to the area pawn shops to ask them to keep an eye out for his photo equipment. We found a list and photos of all his equipment in an insurance folder in his office this morning. There are five cameras unaccounted for."

"Five, wow. So you went back?"

"Yeah, I also caught the neighbor at home. Not a very pleasant guy. Apparently he was suing Vanek for damage to his sixty-thousand-dollar fishing boat, allegedly caused by one of his visiting guests ... and lost wages since he takes people out to secret fishing spots for a fee."

"Ouch. So he's a suspect?"

Will brushed an ant off his slacks and shrugged. "He said he's been out of town since Friday morning. I still have to check out his alibi before I take him off the suspect list."

"Thanks for speeding up this investigation by the way." I leaned over and pressed a kiss on his lips. "You're the best."

"Can I have that in writing?" he teased, pulling me in for a longer kiss. When he finally released me, he sighed. "Well, we have a bunch of leads we're following up on, including talking to the real estate agent, whose business card was the lone object in Vanek's car console. Could mean he contacted her recently. Anything that will help us figure out what he's been up to lately will help."

We packed up our stuff and headed back across Beach Drive. I held open the door for Goldie, and Will handed Petey over to me. "I'll pick you up tonight at seven for Rachel's party."

My gut twisted. "Oh yeah, the party ... I forgot." More like tried to block it out.

* * *

"I don't have anything to wear. I should just call and tell Will to go without me." I was sulking at the kitchen counter watching Mallory spoon out Lucky's food as the cat paced back and forth, mewing for her to hurry up. It was good to see Lucky so happy, considering the circumstances we'd found her in. "Patience is still not her virtue, huh?"

"Nope." Mallory placed the bowl on the counter. Lucky started to purr as she ate. "Just wear one of your sundresses, what's the big deal? You've never worried about how you dressed before."

Willow slid into the seat next to me, and the comforting scent of her ginger tea enveloped me.

I sighed. "But you should see this girl, Rachel, the model who's throwing the party. She's perfect and she lives in a bikini. And there will probably be twenty other perfect women there just like her."

"Whoa." Malloy glanced at me sharply. "What's up with the sudden insecurity?"

When I didn't answer, Willow nudged me with her elbow. "Yeah, what's up? You know Will loves you, and he doesn't seem like the kind of guy tempted by shallow beauty."

"I know and you're right, he's not." I leaned back and crossed my arms. "I keep telling myself that, but this new insecurity won't budge. It's so confusing, and I have no earthly idea where it's coming from."

Willow sipped her tea, then said, "Maybe it's actually coming from the fact that you don't feel Will is accepting of all of you. That there's a part of you he doesn't approve of ... and it's not your body."

I lifted my gaze to Willow. She was very perceptive and right as usual.

"That may be true." Mallory's tone softened. "But sometimes dressing up a little helps, too. What time is he picking you up?"

I glanced at the clock. "In thirty minutes."

She clapped her hands. "Well, I'm no miracle worker, but come on, let's see what we can do."

CHAPTER NINE

I could hear the music before we even exited the car. A heavy beat that felt more like punishment to my brain than entertainment. Will and I shared an unsure look after he rang Rachel's doorbell.

The door swung open and Rachel greeted us wearing a black string bikini.

Of course.

"Detective! So glad you could make it." She flashed her hundred-watt smile and waved us in with the hand that wasn't holding a salt-rimmed drink. At least, she waved Will in, I was apparently invisible.

Mallory had lent me one of her more form-fitting little black dresses and fixed my hair and makeup. She thought feeling pretty and girly would make it less painful to be here. It wasn't working. I just felt like I was playing dress up, especially when our hostess was so dressed down.

As Rachel walked us deeper into the house, I forced myself to stop obsessing over her bikini-clad figure. "Party's in the back by the pool. Food and beverages are in the kitchen. Help yourself."

Will glanced around the room. His gaze didn't stop on the half-naked group of young models making their way through the opened sliding-glass doors. I appreciated that. I was getting a better picture of what Rachel meant by "casual dress." It must be code for "as little clothes as possible."

This whole jealously, insecurity thing was so new and so raw, I wasn't sure how to deal with it.

"Actually, I'd like to talk to C.J. first if he's here." Will was all business, which helped.

Rachel shrugged a bare shoulder. "Whatever you need. I'll find him and tell him to meet you in the kitchen. It's the quietest place to talk."

She wasn't kidding. Trays and trays of food sat untouched. The inner walls even buffered the music enough to be tolerable. I helped myself to a coconut shrimp, which tasted like the Revlon Kiss Me Coral lipstick I was wearing. Dropping it in the trash, I searched for water. "We're going to have to eventually go out there, aren't we?"

He smiled, a bit distracted. "Afraid so."

Just then a tall guy with arms like tree trunks, a clean-shaven head, and eyes like a rattlesnake's burst into the kitchen. He took us in with one glance and then lumbered toward Will.

I had to give Will credit for not backing up. He stood his ground and held out his hand. "C.J.?"

The man-tree nodded and shook his hand. A gold and diamond watch gleamed on his wrist.

Did Will cringe? Kinda looked like it.

"Rach said you needed to ask me some questions?"

Wow, he had a deep voice. He would've made a great voice-over for a villain in those comic book movies Frankie had dragged me to. She called them an escape from reality. I often wondered what she'd say if she knew their powers weren't all that unreal. Sometimes I fantasized about showing her my water magick, but I knew nothing good would come of it.

Will pulled a notebook and pen from his back jean's pocket. "I assume you've heard about Peter Vanek's death?"

C.J. crossed his arms and nodded silently.

I eyed the bull tattoo on his left forearm. It had red glowing eyes and blood dripping from its horns. I wondered what kind of meaning that could possibly hold for a person.

"Rachel told us she spent a lot of time with Mr. Vanek. How'd you feel about that?"

He glared at Will. "I didn't like it. Didn't like him."

I guess Will decided to be as straight forward as C.J. was being because he just came right out and asked, "Didn't like him enough to kill him?"

C.J.'s eyes narrowed and his head did a little jerking back thing. "Kill him? Of course not. Wait, he was murdered? I thought he had a heart attack."

I watched Will study him for a moment. I couldn't tell what he was thinking. He was real good at hiding his thoughts and emotions when he was in detective mode. One of his many admirable skills. "That was the initial belief. Now we're not so sure."

"Wow. That's crazy."

C.J. looked sincerely shocked to me. But maybe he was just a good actor. Maybe Will could tell he was lying by which way his eyes moved, or his ear twitched or the light bounced off his head.

I felt a surge of respect for Will as he stayed silent. He was a great detective. He would solve this case and Sylvia would get married. I believed it. I pushed aside the doubt trying to burrow into that belief. Nope. No doubt. We couldn't afford it. We didn't have time for it.

"Anyone else at this party that didn't like Mr. Vanek?" Will finally asked.

C.J. shrugged massive shoulders. "No, I mean not enough to kill the guy."

"Where were you Saturday morning?"

"At the gym around eight. Before that at home."

"Alone?"

"Yeah."

"Which gym?"

"Gold's on 34th."

Will jotted that down in his notebook and then pulled a card from his pocket. He held it out. "If you think of anything else, give me a call."

"Yeah, sure." C.J. slipped the card into his own pocket and did a little salute before lumbering back through the door.

"What do you think?" I asked.

"Not sure. He's only alibied after eight, if he was telling the truth. I'll have to check on that, and we'll have to wait on a more exact time of death." Will glanced around at the food. "You should eat. I've got to interview the people outside. We may be here awhile."

Groaning inwardly, I poured myself a glass of wine instead and pasted on a smile. "After you, Detective."

The band was taking a break when we walked outside. Thank heavens for small mercies. Without the music blaring, sounds of conversation, laughter and splashing from the pool filled the evening air. There were young women and men draped over everything—deck chairs, pool floats ... each other.

I clutched my wine glass like a life raft. I'd never felt so out of place. Not even back in Savannah where they threw eggs at our house.

Will scanned the crowd. "It'll go faster if we split up. Try to start up a conversation about Vanek, and see what comes up. If anyone talks negatively about him, let me know."

"Is it all right if I mention Peter may have been murdered to these folks, too?"

Will nodded. "Sure. Just note their reaction." He dropped a kiss on my forehead and headed into the fray.

I fought the urge to run after him and beg him not to leave me. How pathetic would that be? Besides, I was always bugging him to let me help with investigations and here he was giving me the green light. I should be happy. Instead I just felt anxious. This world seemed more threatening than a jungle to me. How could I trust myself to be objective?

Just go, Darwin. Get it over with.

I took a large swig from my wine glass, waited for the warmth to hit my belly and then pushed myself forward.

I spotted a woman who looked to be about my age, late twenties. She was sitting alone on the edge of a mermaid statue, wearing a sundress that was the same pale yellow color of her hair. A fully dressed woman. Seemed like a safe place to start.

I moseyed over and stood close enough to her to strike up a conversation. "Great party, huh?"

She shielded light blue eyes from the still-bright sky and smiled up at me. "Rachel does know how to throw a party." Then she pushed herself upright and held out a hand. "Daisy Beaumont. Pleased to make your acquaintance."

Ah, southern manners. I felt myself relax as I accepted her offered hand. With a quick glance, I checked for the gigantic engagement ring from my vision. *Nothing.* "Darwin Winters, pleased to meet you, too. Are you from Georgia by chance?"

"I am," she laughed self-depreciatingly. "Darn this accent. It's like gum on my shoe. I just can't shake it, even after lessons. You, too, right?"

"Yeah, Savannah. What brought you to St. Pete?"

She glanced over at the pool as a particularly loud squeal and splash caught her attention. Her eyes softened as she shook her head. "The dream. Just like these girls. Cover of Sports Illustrated, Vogue, whatever ... it's addictive, the thought that someone thinks you're beautiful enough to sell magazines." Her attention turned back to me and just for a second I caught the pain.

A wave of sadness. I let it flow through me and reminded myself it wasn't mine to bear. Though I did wonder where it came from. She may have been pushing thirty, but she was still a beautiful woman. Surely, she hadn't let go of her dream yet.

"I was scouted when I was sixteen and my mother moved us to Miami so I could pursue a modeling career."

"It sounds like she was very supportive."

"Or delusional." She laughed easily then asked, "What about you? Who are you with?"

"Oh, my boyfriend. Over there." I pointed to Will sitting on a lawn chair, chatting with a tall, well-built man with perfect bone structure and dark, shampoo-commercial worthy hair.

She smiled and watched them silently for a good thirty seconds, a dreamy look in her eye. Was she staring at Will?

Stop it, Darwin, you're being paranoid.

Finally, she shook herself free of whatever thoughts had held her and said, "No, I meant which agency?"

I stared at her, trying to figure out what she was asking. "Agency?"

"Yes, you model right?"

I couldn't seem to wrap my brain around the question. Did she just mistake me for a model? I would've laughed hysterically if I could've gotten my mouth to move. Instead, I shook my head emphatically *no*.

A smile pushed up one corner of her mouth, causing a dimple to appear. "Well, you could, you know. Probably better off, anyway. It's a brutal business. Terrible for a girl's self-esteem. In my experience, anyway." She sighed. "Still, hard to give up on a dream."

"I'm sure it is." I watched Will move on to introduce himself to two girls sharing one lawn chair. "I actually co-own a pet boutique on Beach Drive. Darwin's."

"Oh, really? I've just adopted a dog, and I've been meaning to get him in there for a grooming. I've heard nothing but good things about your place. Good for you."

"Thanks. It's been a learning curve but my partner, Sylvia, and I are pretty happy with how things are going." I took another sip of my wine as our conversation petered out.

What now? Guess there was no use beatin' around the bush.

"So, that was terrible about Peter Vanek's death, right? Was he your photographer, too?"

Was that too obvious? Oh well, too late if it was.

She glanced over at me. "Not for my portfolio shots, no. I use Margie Bealle mostly. I just feel more comfortable with a woman doing those. But yeah, terrible." She took a sip of what looked like sparkling water, a lemon slice bumping against her upper lip. Then she glanced up at the sky as a plane flew over. "Peter had a gift for sure. I did use him for some non-modeling portrait needs. Life is just so darn short, you know? You just never know when your time will be up. Gotta enjoy every day to the fullest."

A tall woman with chestnut-colored skin, wearing a gold, cut out one-piece swimsuit approached us. "Daisy! Haven't seen you in ages, love." The two women air-kissed. "Where you been hidin' yourself?"

"Just busy, Malaika." She turned to me, smiling once again. "This is my new friend, Darwin. She co-owns Darwin's Pet Boutique on Beach Drive."

I shook her hand. "Nice to meet you. We were just talking about Peter Vanek, how tragic it was to lose such a talent. Did you use him?"

A long, thin hand moved to her chest as her hazel eyes softened. "Yes, I sure did. I can't believe he's gone." She surveyed the crowd beneath thick, false lashes. "I guess Margie Bealle is going to get some new clients now." Then she leaned in closer to Daisy. "Speaking of, you have her cell number, right?"

Daisy gave her a chastising look, but she held out her hand and let Malaika drop her cell phone into her palm. As she entered Margie's information, I wondered if a sudden windfall of clients would be motive for murder?

"Daisy, would you mind if I got Margie Bealle's number from you, too?" I dug in my bag for my own cell phone. "I have a friend who'd planned on using Peter for her wedding, and now she's stuck without a photographer."

"Oh, I don't think she shoots weddings." Daisy shrugged and then accepted my phone. "But I guess it wouldn't hurt to ask her. I could be wrong."

As she handed me back the phone, I stepped closer to both of them. Time to see their reactions. "You know, I heard the police are starting to suspect Peter didn't actually have a heart attack."

Daisy and Malaika both stared at me, wide-eyed.

Malaika moved her hand to her throat. Then she blinked and swallowed. "What do they think happened to him?"

"They think it's actually lookin' more like a robbery gone wrong or ... murder."

They both would have to be world-class actresses to fake the shocked expressions they now wore.

* * *

I was exhausted by the time I walked into the townhouse that evening. The lights were all on, and Mallory popped up from behind the sofa. Lucky turned to stare at me with a chirp from her queenly position on top of the sofa, her tail flicking in irritation.

I dropped my straw bag on the kitchen counter and scratched Goldie's chin as she greeted me with her usual enthusiasm and then walked over to give

Lucky a chin scratch, too. "What is your crazy mama doin' on the floor, Lucky?"

Mallory pushed herself up. Blowing her hair out of her face, she rested her hands on her hips. "We're searchin' for Petey."

My heart skipped. "What do you mean? He's gone?"

Willow came down the stairs. "Not gone. He has to be here somewhere."

I moved into the living room and stared at the French doors. "Y'all didn't let him outside on the balcony, did you?" A horrifying image of him falling through the rod iron railing gripped my brain before I could stop it.

"No!" Mallory said. "Of course not. We were watching a movie, and he was here sleeping at our feet one minute and then just gone."

"Well, this place does have three-thousand square feet and four bedrooms to hide in." I looked down at Goldie, who was sitting at my feet staring up at me, wagging her tail and grinning. "You know where he is, don't you girl? Goldie, where's Petey? Go find him!"

With a sneeze, she jumped up and trotted over to the kitchen. We all followed her. When she got to the cabinet beneath the sink, where we keep the extra jars of homemade treats, she scratched at the wood door.

"Looks like she wants a treat first," Willow chuckled.

I bent down and opened the cabinet door. There sat Petey with his chewed bear, next to the treat jar, his stubby little tail ticking back and forth. "How'd you get in there?"

I scooped him up and checked him over while Willow and Mallory laughed with relief.

"Better give him a treat. He earned it, the little bugger." Mallory plucked his bear out of the cabinet and held it up with two fingers. "And you need to wash this thing. It's gross."

As we all settled back onto the sofa, Willow asked, "So any luck tonight?"

I shrugged as Petey stretched over my shoulder and nibbled at my ear. "I found out another photographer in the area, Margie Bealle, will benefit from Peter's death by getting his clients. Also, Will was led to a male model who wasn't very happy. Apparently Peter was holding back images from his photo shoot until he got paid. Both have been added to the suspect list. It's just getting frustrating because we're adding more people to the list than we're taking away."

Mallory smirked. "The bright side is you still have six days to figure out what really happened."

I threw a pillow at her and then cradled Petey in one arm. Gently wiping some goo from his eyes, I noticed he was having a hard time keeping them opened. Tired from his adventure most likely. "All right, I'm out. Come on, Goldie, time to hit the sack."

This time it wasn't dreams of Zach causing my fitful sleep. It was my father.

He was underwater, wearing a black suit, his expression grave. He was trying to tell me something. I haven't seen him since I was nine in real life, but I still recognized him in my dreams.

"Father!" Even though I was under water, my breath came easily, my cries echoing like I was in a cavern. "What are you saying? I can't hear you." I pushed myself forward, closer and closer to him as his mouth moved frantically. The water was clear but tinged with a violet light and so ... empty. Where was all the sea life?

There was an uncomfortable tingling feeling in my body as I pushed closer. It almost felt like an electric current was running through the water. Ignoring it, I propelled myself forward.

When I got about ten feet from him, the water grew too uncomfortable to move forward. The sensation of being shocked buzzed through me. I floated there, holding his worried gaze, not sure what to do next. There were so many questions.

He was still trying to tell me something, his hands motioning in frustration. Suddenly sound broke through whatever barrier I'd reached. His words echoed around me. "Darwin! You're ... not ... safe. Wake up!"

A womanly figure darted at me from behind him. Eyes full of rage. Razor-like rows of teeth. Long hair fanned out behind her. Recognition hit me.

Thwap! Her tail came around and smashed into the side of my head.

"No!" Scrambling from beneath the covers and gasping for breath, I blinked hard. Glancing around the room, I struggled to get my bearings. "You're all right, Darwin. It was just a dream."

Just a dream. Just a dream.

But, as Goldie plopped her head into my lap and looked up at me with eyes full of concern, I held my hand to my throbbing cheek and knew the truth. It wasn't just a dream. It was another warning. And another glimpse at my enemy.

CHAPTER TEN

Tuesday morning, time seemed to be moving slower than molasses as I helped customers at the pet boutique. Also, I was feeling guilty. This was supposed to be a fun trip for my sisters and so far it'd been a disaster.

Between customers, I tried to keep myself busy so I wouldn't watch the clock. I'd unpacked our entire stock of new inventory, wiped down every rack, straightened every shirt, collar, can of food and even arranged the homemade treats by color. Then I'd called Will. Left three messages.

I'd wracked my brain trying to come up with something else I could do to help. I mean, for Pete's sake, it was Tuesday. Sylvia's family was booked for a flight back to Portugal bright and early next Tuesday morning. That meant Monday was the last possible day to hold their wedding. I'd have it in my townhouse if I had to, that wasn't the issue. The anxiety was starting to feel like a nest of bothered hornets in my chest.

As I wiped down the plastic pages of the photo album of birthday cakes, the bell over the door signaled a customer. I glanced up. Surprise made my heart trip in my chest. "Sylvia?" I rushed over and wrapped her in a hug. Holy moly, she felt thin and cold.

I stepped back and looked her over.

Her hair was dull and pulled back into a tight ponytail. Her skin was sallow and dark half-moons had formed beneath her chestnut eyes. There was a coffee stain on her cream-colored button-down shirt and sadness emanated from her in a slow, heavy beat.

Not good.

I steadied myself against her sadness. "It's good to see you but ...what in heaven's name are you doin' here?"

She blew out a deep breath. "I have to do something. My family is driving me crazy. Maybe working will take my mind off everything."

"But you don't have any clients booked for this week," I gently reminded her.

Her panicked gaze darted around the boutique as she raked her teeth across a chapped lip. "I can help customers."

"Okay." I wasn't sure it was a good idea for her to be interacting with people in her state, but what could I say? It was her boutique, too. "I think Mrs. Tilley's almost ready. If you want to ring her up, I'll just run Goldie across the street for a quick potty break since you're here."

She nodded stiffly and forced a smile. It looked more like a new crack forming in a crumbling structure.

Not good at all. I hesitated leaving her alone. But, I would only be a minute. What could possibly go wrong?

When I returned, Sylvia was in tears and Mrs. Tilley was patting her hand, trying to comfort her.

Oh boy.

I wrapped an arm around Sylvia's shoulder. "Thanks, Mrs. Tilley. I got it from here." I gave her a wink and led Sylvia over to sit at the tea table.

"*Desculpa*," she sniffed, plucking a Kleenex from the box next to the hot water dispenser. "I'm sorry. I thought I could keep my mind off Landon and the wedding if I stayed busy."

Goldie trotted over and rested her head in Sylvia's lap. She hated to see anyone upset.

Sylvia stroked my dog's head absentmindedly. "What am I going to do?"

I unwrapped a left-over cherry tart and offered it to her. She shook her head.

Sylvia turning down a dessert? She was in worse shape than I thought. I wrapped the tart back up, much to Goldie's disappointment. Maybe talking about it would help. "Can I ask you something?"

She rested her chin on her fist. "*Si.*"

"How do you know Landon's *the* one?"

Sylvia stared at me and then twisted in her seat. Then her attention shifted to the engagement ring on her finger. "I think you just love someone so much, you hope they are the one."

She settled back into the chair and looked out the window. Her voice was hoarse as she said, "That first day Landon came into the boutique, he was so charming, so intense. I felt an immediate draw to him."

I smiled. Yeah, I remembered that day well.

"But when I knew I loved him … that was two months later. When I had bronchitis, remember?" She glanced at me. I nodded. "He made me homemade chicken noodle soup. His grandmother's recipe. Brought it to my house." Her eyes lit up at the memory. "He stayed even after I fell asleep on him. But, he didn't know I wasn't quite asleep when he whispered, 'How did I get so lucky?' You see? I knew then that I was the lucky one." She blew her nose. "He accepts everything about me ... even my crazy family." She shrugged. "Don't you feel like that with Will?"

I smiled. "Sure." But there was one difference. Will doesn't accept everything about me.

Speaking of ... the bell clanged over the door. I turned to see Will walk in.

"Be right back." Tripping over my own feet, I hurried to him. "Do you have something? Please tell me you have something."

He shifted his weight onto one foot and did a double take when he saw Sylvia. "How's she holding up?"

"She'd be better if she had some good news."

Sylvia got up and came over, looking hopeful. "Is there news?"

"I think I have something. Not sure what it means yet." Reaching down, he stroked Goldie's head as she waited patiently for his attention. "I got ahold of the real estate agent, Betsy Mills. She confirmed Vanek called her last Friday. He told her he was about to come into a lot of cash and asked her to start looking for property that was zoned for the no-kill shelter he wanted to build."

"Yeah, Charlie had told me about the shelter. Coming into a lot of cash though?" I worked that around in my brain, trying to see where it fit. There weren't enough pieces yet to fit anywhere. "How much money are we talkin' about?"

"Don't know. I'll have our guys check into his finances today. I did notice the blueprints for a shelter on his desk, but I have no idea how much money it would take to build it. Guess that's a question that needs answering, too."

I rubbed my arms. "Okay. Well, that's something. But it still wouldn't explain his missing cameras or laptop."

"He could have sold the laptop and cameras maybe," Sylvia said.

"I don't think so," Will answered. "That wouldn't even be a drop in the bucket of what he'd need for the shelter."

Sylvia looked drained. She squeezed my arm. "I'm going to go. This was a bad idea."

"Sure, hon. I'll call you later."

After she left, Charlie came in, looking a bit more disheveled than usual, her pink hair tucked under a Tampa Bay Rays baseball cap.

"Hey, Charlie."

"Hey, guys. I just saw Sylvia. She looked terrible."

"Yeah, she's not doing too good," I agreed. "Hopefully something breaks soon. What are you up to today?"

"I was just at the shelter, trying to get some good shots of the new dogs. Pete made it look way easier than it is." Her head dropped. "I'm still glad to help, but it's just not the same without him there."

I didn't realize she'd gotten so close to Peter. "I'm sorry. You know my grandma says nothing in this world is ever lost. Just changed. Peter's still with you, you may just have to be a little quieter, concentrate a little harder to feel him."

She swiped at a rogue tear. "Thanks, Darwin. Your grandma sounds like a smart lady." She glanced over at Will. "Anything I can do to help figure out what happened?"

"I don't think so," Will said gently. "Appreciate the offer, though."

I watched her shoulders fall. She really wanted to help. "Hey, did Peter mention anything to you about coming into a lot of cash to build that shelter?"

Charlie bit her lip and shook her head. "Nope. But he had started a Fund-Me page a while back for it. Maybe someone was giving him money through there?"

Will perked up. "That's one of those online sites, isn't it? Where people can donate to a cause? Can you show me his page?"

"Sure." She led us over to the computer on the counter and typed something in the address bar. "Here you go."

Will and I leaned over as he scrolled through. I could feel his disappointment. "Looks like he has eight backers and a little over three thousand dollars. Not enough to buy land for a shelter."

"Maybe someone told him they were going to back him and didn't follow through?" I took over the mouse and clicked on the backer names. There were two I recognized. Rachel Jennson and Malaika Diya. They each gave five hundred dollars. "Rachel and Malaika were both Peter's clients. You said Rachel doesn't have a motive, but she doesn't have an alibi, either. And what about Malaika? She was one of the models I talked to at Rachel's party."

Will shook his head and blew out a breath. "Can you print out that list of names? I'll have her checked out along with the other backers." He kissed the top of my head. "All right, time to work. I'll call you if I find out anything else."

"What now?" Charlie asked after Will left.

Something else was bothering me. "Remember when Frankie read us something in the paper about Helping Paws Rescue being investigated for fraud? Something about their mobile spay and neuter program? What if Peter knew something fishy was going on there, maybe saw or overhead something, and confronted the director with what he knew? I mean, he spent enough time there that if something was going on, he'd have noticed, right?"

Charlie chewed on the inside of her cheek. "I just can't see Sassy cheating the system or being a murderer. She fights for the life of every animal in that place."

"But if Peter was putting her shelter in jeopardy? You never know what people are capable of. They're complicated and some people like animals more than humans."

She stared at me, a bit of suspicion surfacing. "That's certainly true."

I went to find my phone to call Will. "Maybe you should wait to go back to the shelter until I can get Will to talk to her. He can find out if Peter confronted her about the fraud allegations." I listened to it ring. "And see if she has an alibi for the morning Peter was killed."

CHAPTER ELEVEN

Will picked me up on Tuesday after I closed up the boutique and we headed out to St. Pete Helping Paws Rescue. He'd called and made an appointment to talk to Sassy White, but he thought maybe I could poke around and talk to the other employees while he was busy with her. Will asking for my help meant he was getting desperate.

He wasn't the only one.

The front room of the shelter seemed pleasant enough and smelled slightly of bleach. The walls were covered in framed photos Peter had taken of the dogs and a few cats ... though those guys didn't look as amused to be wearing tiaras and feather boas.

No one was manning the high counter with the plastic window so Will knocked on the wooden door to our right.

A middle-aged woman, her dark hair plastered to her face with sweat, opened the door. "Oh hey, you must be Detective Blake?" When Will nodded his acknowledgement, she waved us through. "Sassy's office is there on the right. Go on, she's expecting you."

The sound of barking and the smell of confined dogs hit my senses like a Mac truck.

I tried to breathe through my mouth as I followed Will into the kennel area. He headed for the office.

I was supposed to find employees to talk to, so this lady would do nicely. I cleared my throat to get her attention. "Excuse me, ma'am. Would you mind if I took a peek at the dogs?"

When she glanced at her watch and hesitated, I crossed my fingers behind my back, pushed my guilt into a dark corner and added, "I'm thinking about getting another dog to keep my golden retriever company in the daytime."

She shrugged. "Guess it couldn't hurt none. We don't have any puppies right now, though if that's what you're looking for." She opened a second door and mumbled. "Everybody wants a puppy."

We stepped through the door, and she led me down a concrete-floored hallway. I tried to block out the sad, desperate barking and concentrate on the mission.

Breathe, Darwin. It's not going to do anybody any good if you get upset.

"I'm Rhonda, by the way."

"Darwin. Nice to meet you." I had to raise my voice over the barking. "Actually, a dog already potty trained would be best. I can't do a puppy with my schedule." I felt terrible lying to her and getting her hopes up. I'd have to make amends later somehow. Maybe a generous donation.

As we closed in on the metal cages, most of the barking turned to whining. More heartbreaking but easier to have a conversation. "What if I find a dog I like and he's not neutered, do y'all do that? I saw that van out in the parking lot … the mobile spay and neuter one."

She looked me over, assessing my income level, I guessed. "The mobile unit goes out to low income neighborhoods, which I'm assuming isn't where you call home?"

I shook my head silently.

"In that case, we charge a seventy-five dollar fee for our affiliated vet to neuter upon adoption, which yes, is required."

We were standing in front of the cages now and my heart was cracking wide open. A brown and white pit mix was curled up on a flattened, well-worn pillow in the corner of his concrete cage, just the tip of his tail flicking as he watched us with deep brown eyes. His neighbor was a wire-haired terrier mix, who was jumping and barking at us through the fence. At least he still had hope, still seemed determined to be noticed.

I'd have to make sure I didn't touch any of these guys. Most likely they'd all suffered some kind of recent trauma, and I would break down in a ball of snot and tears if they showed it to me right now. And that would bring my investigating to a grinding halt.

"They do get up-to-date shots when we get 'em in though. In fact ..." She moved down a few cages and put a hand on a fleshy hip. "You said you have a golden, right? We have a golden-mix who came out of our intake isolation facility this morning and is ready for adoption. Her name's Sandy. Sweet as pie, that girl. Dropped off by a lady who's mom had just passed, and she couldn't keep her. Such a shame." She looked me hard in the eye. "She does have blood sugar issues and needs shots a few times a day, so it's gonna be hard to find her a home."

I glanced into the cage she was standing in front of. It was empty.

Rhonda shrugged. "She must be getting her shots now. But, you can bring your dog back and see how they get along."

Oh heavens. What was I doing? I really should've thought this through.

Forcing myself to keep up the charade despite the guilt heating up my face I whispered, "Sure. Okay."

Glancing back at the row of cages behind me, I noticed a large, particularly vocal, black-as-night dog pawing at his gate and wagging his tail. I sighed. "I guess it takes a special person to be able to be around all this heartbreak day after day."

"Well, it helps that we're a no-kill shelter. At least they have a chance at getting a family."

I saw my opening and sprinted through it. "You know, I had a friend who really wanted to build another no-kill shelter in the area. Unfortunately, he passed away recently. Peter Vanek. Did you know him?"

She glanced sharply at me, tears suddenly glistening in her large doe eyes. "Sure I knew him." Clearing her throat and swiping at her nose, she stuck her hand against a cage to let the terrier lick her palm.

"Sorry," I said. "I didn't mean to upset you. Did you know him well then?"

Rhonda waved a hand. "Don't mind me. It's just been a long day. I knew him well enough. He took some great photos of the dogs. Dressed 'em up real cute in bandanas and stuff to help 'em get homes. I couldn't believe it when Sassy told me he'd had a heart attack. He seemed like such a health nut, always carrying around some weird green drink. Guess you never know. When your time is up, it's up."

"Yeah." I paused a beat, so I didn't seem so anxious when I asked, "So, Peter and Sassy White got along?"

She shrugged thoughtfully. "Sure ... as much as Sassy gets along with anyone, I guess. Don't get me wrong, she keeps this place runnin' drama-free which ain't easy. But she's all business, getting along isn't her priority."

A door shut somewhere behind us, and we turned to see a tall, handsome man with dark hair and olive skin round the corner. He was dressed in blue scrubs. A spark of recognition stirred in my brain, but I couldn't place him. A plump, white faced golden-mix was at his side.

"Ah, there's Lincoln now with Sandy, the dog I was telling you about." Rhonda moved back to the empty cage as the pair approached. She held the door opened. "How'd she do?"

"Beautifully. Not even a flinch. She's a sweetheart."

The woman grinned at me, her face lighting up. "Told ya. Want to pet her?"

"Oh." Panic fluttered in my chest and sweat broke out under my hairline. I glanced down at the time-whitened face tilted up at me. Sandy was a lighter color than Goldie and a bit overweight, but lord help me, the same achingly sweet spirit stared out at me from those bright, trusting eyes. I bit my lip, hoping the pain would keep my emotions in check. "I better not today. I might fall in love before I see how my dog reacts to her." That was certainly true.

They both nodded as if this was reasonable, and Lincoln gave Sandy one last pat before he led her back into the cage.

My stomach cramped as I watched her sniff around, turn a few circles and then plop down on the bed in the corner. I could imagine Goldie's face whitening like that as the years passed. What I couldn't imagine was her spending those years in a cage instead of a home. Tears pricked my eyes.

Time to go.

"Well, that was the last dog for today." Lincoln pulled off white latex gloves and shoved them into a black bag. "I'll be back on Saturday."

"All right. See ya, Lincoln, and thanks."

"Yeah, I better let you go, too." I gave Sandy one more longing glance. She deserved a home, and it broke my heart I couldn't give her one.

Or could I? I hadn't really thought about adopting another dog. Maybe ... No. Not with my schedule at the pet boutique and her medical needs. I would try to find her a home though, I silently promised her that.

I tuned back in as Rhonda was saying, "Just give us a call and schedule a time to bring your dog in."

"I will. Thanks again."

Lincoln held the door for me, and then we walked back out into the hallway together.

A petite African-American woman with wild gray hair, thick orange-framed glasses and an air of frustration stepped in our path from a side door.

"Lincoln, I have a bone to pick with you." Her hand was on her hip as she eyed me with a raised brow. "How many girlfriends do you have?"

"What's up, Sassy?" He shot me an apologetic look.

I stifled a grin. I could see why Charlie found it hard to imagine this woman committing murder. That would require deception, and she seemed like the "lay it all out in the open" type.

I excused myself and pushed through the door to the front room.

Will was waiting there, his hands in his pockets, staring at a photo of a bulldog in a top hat and bow tie. When he heard me come through, he turned.

"How'd it go?" I asked.

Before he could answer, Sassy and Lincoln came through the door behind me, laughing about something. I guess they worked out whatever she'd been upset about.

Sassy patted Will's arm as she walked by him. "Have a good evenin', Detective. Time to get my old bones home." She pushed the door opened with a hip, letting in the balmy evening air and called back, "I'll see you Saturday, Lincoln."

"Later." Lincoln stopped when he saw Will and held out his hand. "Detective Blake, right? From Rachel's party last night."

"Guilty." Will glanced down at Lincoln's scrubs. "A model and a ...vet?"

"Vet tech," Lincoln corrected him with an amused grin. "More work, less money."

Yeah, now I remembered seeing Will chatting with him at the party while I was talking to Daisy Beaumont. I held out my hand and introduced myself. "I'm Darwin by the way. Nice to meet you."

"Likewise," he said, his smile genuine. "So, you're looking for a dog? Sandy's got a great temperament."

Will saved me from having to lie again. "Actually we're here as part of the investigation into Peter Vanek's death. I know I already asked you about any enemies he might've had, but I just found out Mr. Vanek had plans to build another shelter in the area. So now I'm wondering if there was any conflict between him and Sassy over it. Did you ever see them arguing?"

Lincoln's amused grin resurfaced as he glanced at the door she'd just exited. "I mean, yeah, but Sassy busts everyone's chops. It's just her way. I don't think there was any real conflict or else Pete just wouldn't have come back here, right? He was under no obligation to." He shifted the black bag in his hand. "Look, I've been here twice a week for five years and Sassy's become like an aunt to me … a cranky aunt, but family nonetheless. She wouldn't hurt anyone."

"So, that was a pretty convincing speech Lincoln gave," I said, once we were back in the sedan and buckled in. "Did you get the same feelin' from Sassy when you talked to her, that she wouldn't hurt a fly?"

Will shifted the car into drive. "She didn't seem to be hiding anything, and she has an alibi for part of Saturday morning. Says she'd arrived at the shelter around nine that morning, and it could be verified." He scrubbed his short-cropped hair roughly and then let his hand drop back onto the steering wheel. "So basically, I'm going to have to push the M.E. a bit. Until we find out a more exact time of death, she's still on the hook."

"If Peter died earlier than nine a.m.?"

"Exactly."

I eyed the spay and neuter van, parked in the far corner of the parking lot, as we drove by and wondered if there was any truth to the allegations of fraud connected to their mobile program. "Did you ask her about the fraud charges?"

"I did. She said it's all a mix-up because her employees didn't fill out the state forms correctly. That plus she claims the van was down for a week with a transmission problem. Says it'll all be cleared up soon."

"Do you believe her?"

"Can't say. I don't have enough information."

We stopped at a traffic light. I watched a guy on a bike cross the street in front of us. The sky was starting to soften and turn pink.

"Charlie told me Peter said something about the van not moving, just sitting there all day. Maybe it was really broken down. Maybe not. But, I remember from the paper that it was volunteer staff who brought up the accusations. Peter was a volunteer … maybe he was one of the people accusing her. There's motive. Also, what about Peter wanting to build another shelter? Did she know about that?"

"She did. But she said the more the merrier. They were already turning animals away so she'd be glad to have someone else step up and help."

I stared out the window. "So, now what?"

"Now I go pay a visit to the M.E. and see if we can't nail down a time of death. Hopefully something will turn up in Peter's finances that will tell us where he thought this new windfall of cash was coming from. Money is always a safe bet for motive."

"Or maybe someone will just walk in and confess," I sighed.

A girl can dream, right?

Speaking of dreams. I had a hard time falling asleep that evening. Around midnight, I gave up trying and scooped up Petey, carrying him down the stairs with Goldie at my heels.

My plan was to take the dogs for a walk to clear my head, but when I got to the bottom of the stairs, I realized I wasn't the only one suffering from insomnia. My sisters were huddled up on the couch. Even in the dark I could see something was terribly wrong.

CHAPTER TWELVE

"What's going on?" I stood in front of them, my heart in my throat, glancing from one sister to the other.

Mallory blew her nose into a Kleenex. Her long hair was piled up on top of her head, and she was wrapped in a fluffy pink robe. Lucky was curled up in her lap. "We're just having a little bit of a hard time sleeping what with the crazy woman stalking us in our dreams." Her voice rose at the end.

I stopped breathing. I looked from her to Willow. "Both of y'all?"

Willow nodded. She was facing me, but her attention was directed inward. "We were there together, me and Mal. A shared dream. Father was there, too, in this underwater world. He was trying to warn us about something. He seemed frantic, but neither one of us could hear what he was trying to say."

Anger lit a fire in my gut. It was one thing when I felt threatened, but now this woman was threatening my sisters? I stroked Petey's silky hair to calm myself down. He'd worked his way up to snuggle against my neck, and his warm breath against my skin helped keep me calm. "All right. Make some tea. I've gotta take the dogs out since I woke 'em up, but then we're going to sit down and figure this out."

The park was all shadows and rustling sounds. A thick layer of clouds blocked the moonlight, making it darker than usual. I felt exposed and encouraged the dogs to hurry while I kept an eye on the Bay waters.

Water had always been my ally, but at the moment, it felt like a threat. Like it would spit that crazy woman right out of its depths at me.

Was this her intention? To take away my sense of security? Anger roiled in my gut once again.

A shadow shifted beneath the banyan tree.

"Zach?" I called, my voice amplified by the quiet evening. Nothing. Would he even show himself if he were there?

A cold chill ran up my spine. The urge to flee engulfed me. "Goldie, come." Scooping up Petey, I hurried the three of us back across the street, forcing myself not to look back.

Mallory was seated at the kitchen counter when I walked in, using her magick absentmindedly to stretch a candle flame toward the ceiling then pull it back to a tiny speck of orange light on the wick.

Willow busied herself pouring boiling water from the teapot over diffusers in three clear glass mugs. "I used the oolong," she said distractedly. "I hope that was all right."

"That's fine."

I put Petey on the floor and he began to jump up, trying to bite Goldie's wagging tail while she had her head in the water bowl. When she was done, she turned around and play bowed then took off into the living room with Petey in hot pursuit.

Oh to be a dog.

I glanced at the clock. Almost one in the morning. We were going to be dragging tomorrow. I slipped onto the stool beside my baby sister. Her nose was still red. "So, Mal, you go first. Tell me exactly what you saw in the dream."

There was still a tremor in her voice when she spoke. "It wasn't a dream. It felt too real."

I listened quietly for twenty minutes as they recalled their experience. It was eerily similar to mine. They were in the same underwater world, empty of sea life and tinted with a violet light. The crazy woman with the long hair was there. She'd come at them in a threatening manner, too. Father seemed trapped, unable to help and frantically trying to tell them something. The only difference was I could hear him. They couldn't.

Mallory stifled a yawn and then said, "Maybe your water magick had something to do with you being able to hear Father?" She finally had some color back in her face.

Willow, always the calm, logical one, was making me nervous. I noticed a tremor in her hand as she lowered her teacup.

She glanced up and met my gaze. Worry pinched her brows together. "We should call Grandma Winters. It's time we knew more about what happened to Father. If Mom won't tell us, maybe she will."

Mallory and I eyed her silently. She was right, of course. But Mom would not be a happy camper. She had forbidden us from questioning Grandma Winters about Father's fate. We thought maybe she was just protecting us because we wouldn't ever see him again and needed to move on.

But the fact that Zach had told me Father had been imprisoned—and our dreams seemed to confirm that—I was starting to think these dreams were actually visits. We were visiting him or he was visiting us. Who knows? But it was time for us to get some answers.

I reached across the counter and squeezed Willow's hand. "Can you give Grandma Winters a call in the morning?"

Willow nodded.

I turned to Mallory. "Can you open the boutique by yourself in the morning? I'm going to talk to Zach and find out what else he knows."

"Sure but Darwin ... he's just as big a threat. Are you sure it's worth it?"

I thought about the last time I was in the condo with him. She had no idea what kind of danger he was to me, but I was beginning to understand. "He won't hurt me, Mal. And he knows more about Father than he's told me so far."

"You don't think he's just telling you he knows something to keep you coming back to him?" Willow asked.

I shook my head. "No, I don't think he's lying to me."

"Okay then, we have a plan. Let's try to get some sleep." Willow put her cup in the sink and we trudged back up the stairs with the animals.

I knew I wasn't going to be able to sleep so I put Petey in his crate. Goldie jumped up on the bed, flopped down and stretched out. I rubbed her belly. "You keep Petey company, girl. Momma's got some practicing to do."

I opened the door to the third spare bedroom. The room which held my book, personally-tuned chalice, crystals and other essentials for my practice. Sighing, I whispered, "I'm sorry, Will." No matter how much this might separate Will and I further, it was time.

* * *

Turned out, I didn't have to go far to find Zach. He was waiting for me when Mallory and I exited the gate and walked the few feet to the boutique Wednesday morning. His imposing figure—dressed in jeans, a gray t-shirt and black cowboy boots—lounged against the stucco wall.

Goldie trotted over and sat in front of him, her tail swishing the cement, eyes squinting up happily. I remembered Lucky's complete opposite reaction to him. Guess it was only cats that didn't like him. Or maybe just one particular cat.

He kneeled down and gave her a good rub beneath the ears and then tilted his head up to look at us. "Darwin, I'm not trying to ambush you here, but we need to talk. Hey, Mallory."

Mallory took Goldie's leash from me, ignoring Zach. "I'll take the dogs across the street."

Zach stood and smirked at her exit. "Not a fan?"

I unlocked the door and then turned to watch my sister make her way across the street to the park. The gray Gulf water beyond the park seemed cold and menacing. Uneasiness rippled through me. "Let's chat inside."

Tossing my bag on the tea table, I glared at Zach. I didn't know why I was so angry at him, besides the whole dream invasion thing. Probably making me rely on him for information when all I wanted was him out of my life.

Do you really? A little voice asked in my head.

I ignored it. "Have a seat. I'll be right back."

I went and turned on the lights and the air conditioning, then booted up the computer. By the time I was finished, Mallory was back with the dogs.

I slid into the chair across from Zach. Goldie came and stretched out at my feet beneath the table. "So talk. What do you know about my father?"

His expression was no longer guarded. His dark eyes bore into mine, holding them unapologetically. "Ash Winters." He paused, his head tilted. "He left his world without permission because he fell in love with the human race, became obsessed with their innocence and ability to love despite the horrors they inflict on each other. This is apparently a weakness for them ... human love." His eyes sparked and the intensity of his gaze flared. He shifted his focus out the window instead of at me and continued. "And then he fell in love with one particular human. Your mother. Your father's kind are allowed to interact, to observe but they are also warned—don't interfere, don't get involved, don't change the balance of your world. Their power can wreak too much havoc on your delicate balance here. But, he didn't listen."

I was struggling to follow him and process what he'd just said. "So, you're saying in this other world, where our father's from, everyone is an elemental like us?"

Mallory had stopped cleaning the counter and was very still, listening.

Zach shook his head, finally turning back to me, his eyes widening slightly at my question. "Have you not been told about your ancestry by now?"

I shook my head and held my breath. I knew Father was from another world, but I had no idea what that meant exactly. *Did Zach know? Would he tell me?* I let my eyes do the pleading, afraid my voice would fail me.

He watched me for a moment and then nodded. "Very well. You should know. Your father comes from *Sidhe* or the Otherworld. A parallel dimension of gods, immortals and magic."

"*Sidhe*." I tried the name out on my tongue. It felt good. "So, is our father immortal?" I whispered, almost choking on the revelation.

"No. He can live a long life, but he can also be killed like any other mortal. His is a race the Irish legends called *Tuath De'* and later *Fae*, though they call themselves neither. His race is gifted with certain abilities to manipulate the energies of nature, which serves a particular function to keep their world in balance, but his gifts work differently here. They are more powerful and can cause disruptions. It's why your father could work true magic here, but it's also why it's punishable for *Tuath De'* to mix with mortals. His disobedience wasn't discovered until after he had already returned many times and fathered the three of you."

"Lucky for us," I whispered. "But, wait ...What about his mother? Is Grandma Winters from this Otherworld, too?"

"Yes, but she's not his real mother, in the sense that you're used to. Once he fathered the three of you, she was sent to watch over you, a guardian of sorts to make sure your inherited gifts didn't upset the balance. From what I've been able to gather, when a *Tuath De'* mates with a human, the offspring receive a small part of the *Tuath De'* abilities, an elemental gift—the ability to control earth, fire, water or air. They may also come with other subtler side effects, like your energetic connection with animals."

And also feeling strong human emotions.

"She was to teach you how to use these gifts so you didn't hurt yourselves or others. Also so you would understand how important it was to keep them hidden. But your father had to be punished for his rule-breaking. He was brought back to his world and imprisoned."

"Yeah, we think he's in some kind of underwater prison. How long will they keep him there?"

"That I don't know."

My head was whirling with the new information. It felt like Christmas. "We've all dreamed about him, but we think they were actually visits. That's possible, right?"

Zach cocked his head thoughtfully. "Yes. There are doors from *Sidhe* to this world. Dreams, trances, a few physical spots where the membranes are thin enough to slip through ... if you know where they are. Which I don't."

But he knew how to slip into my dreams. A combination of embarrassment and anger rushed heat to my face. "Dreams seem to have a lot of unwanted doors." I leaned back in my chair, putting distance between us, and crossed my arms.

He nodded but instead of looking apologetic, he leaned toward me on the table. "The open state while dreaming allows for a connection with the universal consciousness. All doors are open. It's a vulnerable time. And—" he flattened his hands on the table. And there it was finally—the remorseful look I'd been waiting for. "I'm truly sorry if you feel I took advantage of that. The truth is I don't have as much self-control there as I do here."

That makes two of us.

His hands opened. "Forgive me?"

I glared at him, but realized I did forgive him. "Sure. Just try harder not to ... butt into my consciousness."

Relief softened his face. "You have my word."

Sweat prickled my neck. He still felt dangerous to me. Time to change the subject. "Why are you telling me all this now?"

He sat back in the chair. "I saw the threat through my own dreams. You're in danger, all of you. That's what I needed to tell you. I'm not sure why, but there's a hatred pointed in your direction from *Sidhe* like a missile. In my own dreams, I only see pieces of the threat. Its eyes, a mouth full of rows of shark-like teeth, razor blade tail like some weaponized mermaid."

I went still inside at his description. It had to be the same woman we'd all seen.

"A rage burns deep within her. I ..." He seemed unsure of himself for the first time. "Darwin, I don't know if I can protect you from her."

My body went cold at his fear and my memory of her manifesting in the Gulf, but I straightened my back and shoulders. "I can protect myself."

The corner of his mouth twitched. Was he amused? He better not be laughing at me. I felt the heat rise in my cheeks.

But the look he was giving me now was too intense to be mistaken for amusement. "Are you still shunning your gift?"

I wanted to say that it was none of his business, but I found myself suddenly too tired and too in need of an ally. "I've started practicing." Though, from my efforts last night I had a long way to go to be able to control it. I was definitely rusty.

His chin dipped once. "Good." He took a deep breath and slid out of the chair. "I'll let you know if I find out anything else. Be careful." Then he added sheepishly, "Please."

"Zach, one more question."

He nodded.

"Why are *you* dreaming about her ... about the threat to us?"

"Because, Darwin, we're connected." His dark, liquid gaze held mine as a sad smile pulled at one corner of his mouth. "I am bound to you."

I watched him disappear through the door, stunned by his words. Bound to me? Could what Willow told me about jinn be true? Her words came back to me:

One thing I do know is when jinn fall in love, they become sort of a slave... bound to that person's desires, to help them out in their life.

The soaring heat rushing through my body only confused me, angered me. It felt a lot like joy. I squeezed my eyes closed. "Stop it. Stop it. Stop it." Once I felt more under control I turned to face my sister, hoping she didn't hear that last part.

So, what did you think of all that?" I asked Mallory.

She was kneeling on the floor, trying to slip Petey's tiny legs through a t-shirt while he gnawed on her finger. When she glanced up, her green eyes were slick with tears. "Why couldn't Mom just explain that all to us? Why couldn't she tell us about that other world and where our gifts came from? Why did we have to hear it from a stranger?"

Petey squirmed and rolled over on his back. Mallory scratched his pink belly and then leaned over and kissed his nose, her tears falling into his fur.

My first reaction was to defend Zach. He wasn't exactly a stranger. Instead, I crossed my arms. "I don't know, Mal. But you can bet whatever her reasons were, they weren't to hurt us. She obviously thought she was protecting us."

"Well, that didn't work, did it?"

I knew she was thinking about the crazy woman stalking us. I could feel the anger in her words. I went to the back to check my supply of flower essence, deciding to leave her to work it out herself. We would all have to do that.

A heaviness had lifted off my heart. I stared at the brown glass flower essence bottles, labeled and lined up on the shelves, trying to figure out why. And then it hit me. I'd always wondered if our gifts had come from a place of good or evil. Knowing that they were just a result of our unique genetics and not from the devil or any of the other things people believed, well ... it felt good. I didn't feel like such a freak. And it suddenly seemed wrong to shun that part of myself. After all, if I couldn't even accept all of me, then how could I expect Will to?

CHAPTER THIRTEEN

I was still in a good mood when Mrs. Fieldsman came in an hour later to order a birthday cake for her elderly Dashhound.

"What's in this one, dear? Peanut has a gluten allergy, you know." Her gnarled hand shook as she pointed to a bowl-shaped cake.

"No problem, Mrs. Fieldsman. I only use coconut flour since gluten can be a problem for a lot of dogs. Besides the flour, that particular cake is made from shredded carrots, peanut butter, eggs, baking soda, coconut oil and a splash of vanilla."

Mrs. Fieldsman chuckled. "Well, that sounds good enough to share with her."

I grinned. "That part you actually could eat. Though, I do fill the bowl with some high quality dog kibble, so you might want to skip that."

Her watery blue eyes were full of good humor as she winked at me. "Thanks for the advice. I guess I'll take it in the pink. Can you have that delivered Saturday morning? I'm having her party at noon."

"Yes, ma'am."

As I was about to fill out the order, the bells over the door jingled. I glanced up. It was Will and he did not look happy.

"Hey, Mal?" I called.

She peered around the corner of the cat aisle. "Yeah?"

"Can you finish up Mrs. Fieldsman's cake order for me?" I jerked my head toward Will, who was pacing in front of the leashes hanging on the wall.

"Yeah, sure." She hurried over, getting the hint.

"Thanks. Pink bowl. Delivery for Saturday morning." I moved to Will's side. Looking up at him, the tension in his face was obvious. "What's going on? Did something happen?"

He dropped a distracted kiss on my cheek, and then rubbing his own forehead roughly he said, "Yes. The M.E. pinned down time of death to around nine a.m., give or take a half an hour. He also got the toxicology test results back from the FBI crime lab this morning. They confirmed his suspicion that Vanek was killed with succinylcholine. Sux is a fast-acting muscle relaxant that paralyzes the respiratory muscles. Anesthesiologists use it." Will's eyes flashed with a fresh, bright anger. "So he would've been aware, awake but unable to move while he suffocated to death."

My hand flew to my mouth. No wonder Will was so agitated. "That's just awful. Who would do something like that?"

His jaw muscles tightened as he glared at the wall of leashes, not seeing them. "That's what I'm going to find out."

I paused, letting the waves of anger, both mine and Will's move away before I asked, "How easy is it to get this drug? Can you just order it over the Internet?"

He nodded and his troubled gaze met mine. "You can probably order anything over the Internet. But most likely, the killer got it from a local hospital, doctor's office ... or vet clinic."

He reached out and pulled me into him. His body shuddered, and then he steeled himself once more before releasing me.

Warmth flooded my body as I realized he did actually lean on me for support. Maybe he even needed me. My heart swelled with love for him. I wrapped my arms around his waist and pressed into him one more time. I couldn't help myself.

"Hey, you okay?" He asked as I pulled away.

My chin tilted up, I nodded and gave him a reassuring smile.

"All right. I'm heading over to the Southern Cross Clinic now to have a chat with Dr. Marisol Olivero. They provide the vet care for Helping Paws Rescue. Sassy White and her shelter seem to be connected to Vanek's death somehow, so I'm starting there."

That was really only a hunch, but it was all we had. I gave his hands an encouraging squeeze. "I know finding out how Peter died is just awful news, but knowing does bring us one step closer to putting this killer behind bars where he belongs, doesn't it?"

"Hopefully." Lifting one of my hands, he pressed a kiss on my palm. His shoulders sagged beneath his jacket, and he suddenly looked beat. "Landon called me last night, wanted to know how the investigation was going. He sounded really ... down."

I nodded. "They both are." Then I thought of something. "You know what? I'm going to give Sylvia a call. Maybe just knowing Peter had this sux drug in his system will be enough evidence of foul play for her mother to give her blessing now."

He forced a sad smile. "That would be the rational thing for her to do."

I sighed. *He's right. Rational isn't in the building.* I had to try anyway.

I was getting ready to leave a message when a breathless Sylvia picked up. "I'm here. You have news?"

"Yes." Finally, I could say yes. "I do. It's good and bad. Will just stopped by. Peter had a drug called sux in his system. It's a fast-acting muscle relaxant that paralyzes the respiratory muscles. Anesthesiologists use it, which is the bad news. He...he suffocated to death."

A gasp from Sylvia's end. "That is awful. *Pobre homem.*"

"I know, it is awful. Will's more determined than ever to find the person who did this. But, the good news is it does prove that Peter didn't die from natural causes. Do you think it's enough for your mother to give her blessing now?"

"*Eu não sei.* Hold on. She is here."

I listened as Sylvia explained the new information to her mother. I didn't understand the words, but I did hear the hope in her tone. After a moment of silence, that changed. Her voice began to rise. I could hear her mother's voice rising in the background, too. I bit my cuticle. What in the world were they saying? It was definitely starting to sound like an argument.

Sylvia came back on the phone with a growl. "My mother, she thinks you make this up to trick her into giving her blessing. Only an arrest for the murder of Peter Vanek would convince her that this wasn't God's will."

I refrained from banging my head on the counter, but just barely.

* * *

I sat on the edge of the sofa after dinner, with Lucky stretched out behind me, purring loudly. Willow sat on a footstool in front of me while I brushed her long hair until it shined, like I used to do when we were kids. It was soothing to both our nerves. Mallory was sprawled out on the floor playing with the dogs.

Mallory and I had just finished explaining to Willow everything Zach had told me about *Sidhe* and Father being *Tauth De'* and how Grandma Winters wasn't really our grandma but our guardian of sorts, which made our relationship with her make much more sense. Her short visits, her obsession with our gifts, even Mom's attitude toward her, which was more reverence than warmth.

We were trying to figure out what our next move should be.

"Well, if she's truly our guardian," Willow said, "it doesn't make me feel any better that she sounded so worried today when I finally got ahold of her."

"She sounded worried?" Mallory pushed herself up on one elbow. "You didn't tell me that." Petey jumped into the cascade of auburn hair falling down her shoulder. "Ouch!" She worked to get it from his teeth. "She's never seemed worried about anything."

"Yeah, which is why I didn't want to tell you," Willow said.

"What exactly did she say?" I put the brush aside and started to French braid her hair.

Willow shrugged. "Not much. She said she had to look into things, and she'd get back to us as soon as she could. It was just the way she said it that bothered me."

Mallory tossed Goldie's stuffed gator across the room. Goldie pounced on it. "Maybe we should call Mom." She sounded like a scared thirteen-year-old girl again.

My heart went out to her.

"You know that would just freak her out, Mal," Willow said gently. Our mother did not handle stress well. "Grandma Winters will know what to do."

After I was done with Willow's braid, I sipped my tea and watched the dogs.

Petey had latched onto the gator in Goldie's mouth and was shaking his head back and forth, growling a tiny puppy growl. Goldie held her head down, her tail slowly arching back and forth. My heart swelled with affection. For her to share her favorite toy with Petey ... she could teach us humans a thing or two about getting along.

Mallory tossed Petey's stuffed bear up into my lap. "While he's occupied, you should wash this. Seriously, it stinks to high heaven."

Putting my tea cup down, I picked up the tiny stuffed bear, stiff with saliva, and grimaced. It was pretty disgusting. I squeezed its belly. There was something hard inside it. A squeaker? If it was, it no longer worked. I felt around the edges of it. It was long and square. "There's something in here. I should probably remove it before it goes in the washer," I said absentmindedly, my thoughts still on the danger we were in.

"How does Zachary Faraday know about Father anyway?" Willow asked. She sounded lost in her own thoughts, too.

I went to the kitchen to fetch scissors. "He just knows things," I said, returning to my place on the sofa. I carefully snipped the large stitches along the bear's neck. It looked like it had been repaired at one time. "I think it's just part of his jinn nature or maybe he inherited some of his mother's gifts. She was a fortuneteller."

"I forgot he's a hybrid like us." Willow said thoughtfully. "Maybe he's not as dangerous as we think. He does seem to be protecting us."

"Grandma Winters thinks he's dangerous, remember?" Mallory asked. Her green eyes flashed with irritation as she glared at me.

Yeah, I remembered the message she'd passed to me through Mallory. *Zach sounded like jinn and jinn were dangerous. Stay away from him.*

I shrugged and moved my attention back to the dog toy. "But if she knew him personally, she might think differently. He's done nothing but help us." I made the hole just big enough to jam my pinky down into the stuffing. It hit a hard object, and I worked it back through the hole.

"That's—"

Willow cut her off. "Mal, she's right. And it's probably a good thing right now that he's looking out for you, Darwin. As much as Will wants to protect you, he's not going to be able to. Not from this crazy fish-woman. How would you even explain this kind of threat to him?"

"I wouldn't," I said, grateful she could see past the whole "jinn" thing and realize how Zach being in our lives wasn't all bad. "I couldn't explain it to Will at all. He'd think I was off my rocker for sure."

That made me sad, but the sadness was shoved to the side to process later because of what I was now holding in my hand.

CHAPTER FOURTEEN

Mallory pushed herself off the floor. "What is that?"

I pulled the cap off the end, my heart racing. "It's a flash drive. It was in Petey's bear."

This must be why Peter had the bear stashed on top his dresser. For safe keeping.

"That means someone hid it there on purpose and that someone was probably Peter! Let's find out why." Mallory raced upstairs and came back down with her laptop.

My hand shaking from adrenaline, I plugged the flash drive into the port.

We watched as Mallory clicked through to open the drive and then clicked on the lone yellow folder. Around two dozen photo icons were displayed. She opened the first one. It was an image of the spay and neuter van in the parking lot of Helping Paws Rescue. She kept clicking. They were all photos of the van, most from kind of far away like surveillance photos. We went back through them again.

"What do you think this means?" Willow asked, leaning over me to get a better view.

"I have no idea." I stroked Lucky's arched back as she walked across my legs to try to get between Mallory and the laptop.

Mallory scooped her up and draped her over a shoulder. She meowed in protest.

I leaned in closer. "They all have time stamps and different dates. Maybe that means something. Maybe Peter was trying to prove the van wasn't actually going out to the low-income neighborhoods like they said they were. That's what they were being accused of, though her explanation to Will was that the van had a transmission problem. If that was a lie, this could be evidence against Sassy White in that fraud case."

"Then why wouldn't Peter just turn it over to whoever was investigating the shelter?" Willow asked, twirling the tip of her braid around her finger. "Why would he hide the evidence?"

"Maybe he was using it against Sassy White somehow," Mallory said.

"Like blackmail?" I rubbed my temple. Trying to get inside someone else's head was making my own head thump. I couldn't even figure out my own motives half the time.

Willow sighed and moved to stretch out on the floor. Goldie stretched out next to her and rolled over for belly rubs. "Blackmail, huh? Hey, didn't you say Peter thought he was going to come into a lot of money? Maybe he *was* getting that money by blackmailing Sassy White with these photos."

I gave her a doubtful look. "Do you know how much shelter directors make? Barely enough to survive. Besides, she wouldn't have any problem supporting another shelter in the area if she had the money. Blackmail wouldn't be necessary. It's not like they're in business competition."

I jerked my foot as tiny teeth sank into my big toe. "Ouch, you little vampire!" I squealed at Petey. Scooping him up, I held him close to my chest. Two shiny eyes gleamed at me mischievously, and then he jumped up and bit my chin. I couldn't help but laugh as I snuggled him into my neck. "And a rascal, too. I think it's time for a potty break."

At the word "potty" Goldie jumped up and headed for the door. I held Petey's little two-pound body in one hand as I dug through my bag for my phone. "I'll call Will and tell him what we found." I was hoping he would've called me already anyway to let me know what Dr. Olivero said.

Willow came up behind me and slipped Petey out of my hands. "I don't think it's a good idea for any of us to be outdoors alone right now. I'm going with you."

"Yeah, you're probably right. Thanks." I snapped on Goldie's leash and handed Willow Petey's harness and leash.

We rode the elevator down and stepped out into the tropical courtyard tucked between two buildings. The sweet scent of summer flowering plants hung in the air.

"Amazing it's still this hot and muggy after the sun goes down, and people still choose to live here," Willow said.

"It's just as hot in the summer back home. Are you tryin' to talk me out of loving this town?" I closed the iron gate behind us and smirked at my sister.

"Why would I do that?" she asked, trying to sound indignant.

I wasn't buying it. "Why indeed."

We made our way across the quiet street. I walked Goldie over to the banyan tree as I dialed Will.

Surprisingly he answered on the first ring. "Hey, I was just getting ready to call you."

That made me feel better. I don't know why I was still so insecure about our relationship ... Well, that wasn't true. I knew why. The big "thing" between us that he was uncomfortable with. The part of me he couldn't accept. It made our connection feel tenuous, like it could dissolve at any moment.

I released this thought to focus on what was important. "I have something for you, but first how did your chat with Dr. Olivero go?"

"Well, I actually just got finished with her at the station. She'd agreed to come in after I asked her if the clinic had any sux go missing. Turned out when she checked for me, there was one 40 mg vial gone. But the problem is ... they just did inventory three days ago and everything was in order, so the vial actually went missing *after* Vanek's homicide."

I stopped walking and let Goldie happily sniff the myriad of scents around the banyan tree. "After? That doesn't make any sense. It's too big of a coincidence to ignore though, isn't it?"

"I think so, yes."

"But you don't think Dr. Olivero had anything to do with it?"

"My gut says no. She was very cooperative, actually seemed really broken up when I told her how Vanek died. But, that doesn't mean someone else in the clinic isn't involved."

I sighed, too drained to even try to put the pieces together.

"So, what did you want to tell me?" Will asked.

"Oh, I found something sewn inside Petey's stuffed bear, a flash drive." A loud splash in the water beyond the park made me jump. I immediately looked for Willow and found her kneeling down next to Petey who was rolling around in the grass.

"A flash drive?" Will's voice rose with surprise. "Did you check to see what's on it?"

"Yeah, photos of the spay and neuter van parked in the Helping Paws lot. They're time stamped, so we figured maybe Peter was trying to get proof of the fraud they were being accused of."

"If he was, why wouldn't he just turn the proof over to the investigators? Why hide it?" Will asked.

"That's what we wondered."

Goldie's ears perked up and she turned toward the Bay. The hairs on my arms rose. I squinted through the dim light for any sign of movement.

"And why would he care?" Will asked. "Maybe someone was paying him to get the proof. Maybe that's where he was getting the money from. Or blackmailing Sassy White?"

I was only half-listening now as a low growl had started in Goldie's throat. I noticed Willow had stood and was facing the Bay, too.

"I'll come by the boutique in the morning and pick up the drive," Will said. "This is big, Darwin. This could be the reason someone stole all Peter's cameras and his laptop ... Maybe they were looking for those photos. We may have motive now." When I didn't answer, he added, "Darwin? You still there?"

I was frozen. A dark shape, a shadow, had lifted, separated from the water and glided effortlessly onto land. "Willow!" I screamed. "Run!"

I pulled Goldie along as she barked, tearing across the road, my conversation with Will forgotten in the terror. My awareness shrank to the pounding in my ears, the strain on my shaking legs.

It took me a few times to slide my gate card with trembling fingers. Finally, mercifully I heard the *click*. I jerked the gate opened and whirled around.

Willow was right behind me. She stumbled in, Petey clutched tight to her chest. I slammed the gate and we both stared in horror at the figure now standing beneath the banyan tree watching us.

A low rumbling reached my ears and the figure stumbled back a few feet as the ground began to shake. Glancing at Willow, I saw my sister's fear had morphed into rage, and she was letting the woman know it, too, as she shook the ground beneath her feet.

The woman turned and disappeared.

I grabbed my sister's arm and we collapsed like wet noodles on the elevator floor, both of us trying to catch our breath.

"Well," I pushed out between breaths, my arms locked around Goldie's neck, "I guess that answers the question of whether she can come after us on land or not."

Willow glanced down at the phone in my hand.

"Oh!" I said, finally registering the sound of Will's muffled voice. I lifted it to my ear.

He was frantically yelling, "Darwin! What's wrong? Darwin!"

"I'm here," I managed. "I'm fine."

"What happened? I heard you scream …"

"I'm fine," I lied. "A stray dog was chasing us in the park, that's all." The tears came then. More from the fact that I had to lie to Will than from being chased by some psycho fish-woman from our father's world. "We're in the house now."

"You scared me."

"Me too," I whispered. "I'll see you in the morning."

I hung up and pressed my face into Goldie's fur.

CHAPTER FIFTEEN

I had stayed up most of the night practicing my water magick and failing miserably to tap into the Original Consciousness that Willow said was necessary to move to the next level.

So it was no surprise when Will tilted my chin up Thursday morning and frowned at the dark circles under my eyes. "You're not sleeping, are you?"

The tears I'd been holding at bay welled up and spilled down my face, and I knew underlying them was the fact I couldn't be honest with him about why I was so tired. Hiding a part of my life from him was painful.

"Sorry," I said, digging for a Kleenex under the counter. I blew my nose and took a deep, shuddering breath. "It's just ... I'm so worried for Sylvia and Landon."

And my family is being threatened by a woman from another world, but that's also my secret to bear.

"We're their only hope of having a life together. I guess the pressure is just starting to get to me. I feel so helpless."

Will folded me into his chest. I let myself sink into him. "Hey, don't lose hope on me now," he said. "I'm narrowing down the suspect list. The neighbor has a solid alibi. He was out of town for two days and that checked out so he's crossed off. The male model whose photos were being held by Vanek for payment was in a car accident the night before he was killed, so the kid was still in the hospital. And besides, we've got a possible motive now and good leads to follow up on today. Who knows what could happen. Our break could come."

He lifted my chin and made me look into his eyes. So blue and sincere. "I've got a list of all the people who had access to sux at Southern Cross, and I'll be interviewing them today. Starting with Lincoln Lee, the vet tech we saw at Helping Paws Rescue. The shelter is connected somehow, I feel it. Especially after you found the flash drive with those photos of their mobile clinic. Just don't give up yet, okay? We still have four days to figure this out so Sylvia and Landon can get married by Monday."

"Four days? That's not a lot of time." I thought for a moment. "Okay. You have the shelter angle covered. But what if we're barking up the wrong tree? What if his death isn't connected to the shelter? Who is the second most likely suspect? If you had more time, who else would you be investigating?"

He rubbed my arms thoughtfully. "I would say the photographer who's inheriting Peter's clients, Margie Bealle. If she did it, it would explain the missing cameras and laptop, tools of her trade that she could use. But ... I have to follow the most likely scenario. Like you said, time is not on our side here."

"Well, that's something I could help you out with. I could go talk to her." I saw his answer in the worried shake of his head. I held up a hand. "Will, I have to do something. I'm going crazy, and she won't even know I'm investigating, I promise. I'll figure out a way to talk to her that won't be about Peter's death."

His eyes registered skepticism but at least he was listening. "How?"

"Well ..." *Come on, Darwin, think.* The idea hit me like a truck. "I got it!" I squealed. "I'll call her as a desperate model who needs pictures immediately or something drastic will happen. I don't know that part yet. But I can do this, Will! Pretty please with sugar on top?"

Like I've said before, not above begging.

He had his arms crossed now and was staring out the window behind me. I could see the struggle on his face. I seemed to be responsible for that expression a lot. I held my breath.

"All right. Just feel her out, get a sense of what type of person she is, if you think she's capable of murder. Also, only bring up Vanek in the sense that he was your former photographer and you're upset about his death. Don't try to ask her any questions about how she felt about him or where she was that morning. Got it?"

I bounced on the balls of my feet and then hugged him. "Got it." And also, I could check her hand for that diamond ring, but I didn't say that for obvious reasons.

He blew out a breath and I noticed the shadowy half-moons under his eyes. He wasn't sleeping either. "It'll be a busy day but let's have dinner after you close up the boutique so we can compare notes."

"Sounds like a plan."

He gave me a kiss and I watched him leave.

I paced the boutique trying to come up with a plausible photo emergency. The one I came up with was pretty lame, but I hoped I could sell it.

I dialed Margie's number and waited. Shoot, I had to leave a message. I closed my eyes and put on my best distraught voice, which came with a heavy dollop of my Georgia accent. "Miss Bealle? Hi, my name is Darwin Winters, and I have a huge emergency I was hoping you could help me out with. I recently had my car stolen with my laptop and modeling portfolio in the trunk. I had all my digital copies on that laptop and was a client of Peter Vanek's so I can't even get more copies from him, may his poor soul rest in peace. I have a huge interview with a potential client on Monday but can't show up without photos!" I sniffled here for effect.

"I know you're in high demand and very busy, but if there's any way you can squeeze me in for a quick photo shoot, I would be forever in your debt. And also I would pay double your fee," I added as an afterthought. Leaving my phone number, I crossed my fingers and toes that I sounded desperate enough.

I carried my phone around as I helped customers the rest of the morning. Why does waiting for a return call make time move slower than a herd of turtles? I tried hard not to think about Sylvia and Landon and what the consequences of our failure to find Peter's killer would mean for them. But it was always buzzing around the back of my mind like a nest of riled up hornets.

At one point I caught Goldie watching me from her position under the tea table. Her brown eyes tracked me with what looked like concern.

She was right. I needed to relax. I took some deep breaths.

Charlie came in around lunchtime to see how things were going. I wondered if she was bored and regretting taking the summer off, or if she just needed to keep busy to keep her mind off of Peter's death. I told her about the drug that was used to kill Peter and that Will was looking into the vet clinic that worked with Helping Paws.

I also asked her to make sure she got a nice photo of the golden-mix, Sandy. She said she thought she already had a photo of her, she'd check.

I felt guilty about lying to the shelter worker and was still entertaining the crazy idea of actually adopting the older dog. The reality was I already had to find one dog a home. Goldie was low maintenance, but there'd be no way I could take care of Petey or a high maintenance dog once my sisters weren't here to help out.

"Hey, I have an idea." I walked over to the blank wall above our bin of homemade treats. "Let's hang up a bulletin board right here. We can post pictures and descriptions of some of the animals you take pictures of. Give them some more exposure to the folks who don't visit the shelter and maybe help them find homes faster."

Charlie clapped her hands. "That's a great idea, Darwin. I'll pick up a bulletin board today and print out some of the photos." She shot back out the door before I could respond.

I smiled to myself. She was definitely happy to have something to do, to keep her mind off losing her friend and mentor, I'd bet.

Mallory and Willow came in with Petey shortly after that, saving me from my obsessive thoughts.

"We brought you something to eat." Willow placed a picnic basket on the table.

"Thanks, y'all," I said, knowing they probably had an ulterior motive of worrying about me being alone. I lifted Petey from Willow's arms. I could barely feel his tiny bones beneath the silky hair. They were like bird bones. "Come here, cutie pie. I need some sugar."

He immediately began trying to eat my face. At least that was what his little tongue-bath and gnawing felt like.

Laughing, I tucked him under my chin. "Mmm, puppy breath. The cure for whatever ails you."

He bit my chin. I was trying hard not to get attached to the little guy, but he was slowly wiggling his way into my heart. Such a little bundle of love.

Goldie pawed at my leg.

"Oh, you missed him, too, huh?" Bending down, I sat him on the floor next to her.

She shoved her nose into his fur, her tail wagging. With a yip, he leaped at her and she hopped towards one of the aisles, looking back and waiting for him to catch up.

I could hear Sarah Applebaum from somewhere down the aisle saying, "Oh, aren't you precious!"

A potential adopter maybe? I filed that question away for when I rang her up.

"I think Goldie believes Petey's her new plaything." Mallory grinned at me while unpacking sandwiches. "She's gonna be real sad when you find him a home."

"That'll be two of us. What is that?" I stuck my finger in the dip Willow had just pulled cellophane off of.

She smacked my hand and handed me a carrot. "Roasted pepper hummus."

I laughed, feeling the pressure escape a little as I smiled at my sisters. It was so good to have them here. I would not be handling this as well without them. "So, any news from Grandma Winters?"

Willow tried to conceal her worry, but I caught it in her tightening lips. "Not yet." Unwrapping a sandwich, she changed the subject, "Any word from Will?"

"Yeah, he came in this morning for the flash drive. He's going to interview the people today who had access to the sux at the vet clinic." I shook my head. "Though it doesn't make sense that some of it went missing *after* Peter was killed."

I bit a carrot and chewed. My brain hurt. My heart hurt, too.

"Will thinks Peter's death is connected to Helping Paws Rescue somehow. I agree, but I'm still going to try to talk to Margie Bealle, the photographer who'll probably get all Peter's clients now. To rule her out if nothing else." I checked my phone. "If she ever returns my call."

"Why is Will so convinced this had something to do with Helping Paws?" Mallory asked. "Just because of the photos on the thumb drive?"

"Most of the evidence can be tied to the shelter somehow. Except for my vision from Petey of the ginormous diamond ring. But, I'm not even sure his brush with whoever was wearing that had anything to do with Peter's death. It wasn't a very traumatic moment for him. More like sad and confusing."

"Maybe he just didn't understand what was happening," Willow offered.

"Probably he didn't."

"So, the big clue is the drug used to kill Peter." Mallory said with a grimace. "What an awful way to die."

"Terrible, yes. That and the other big clue is Peter's missing cameras and laptop."

Mallory licked hummus off of her finger. "Which the killer probably stole looking for the photos stashed on that flash drive. So it has to have something to do with that mobile spay truck."

"Or his stuff could've been stolen by Margie Bealle. It's equipment she can use, so maybe she just couldn't resist taking it after she killed Peter?" My shoulders fell. "Pretty thin, I know."

I startled as my phone vibrated in my pocket. Jumping off the chair I pulled it out and stared at the number. "It's her!" I answered it.

"Miss Winters, this is Margie Bealle. I got your message."

CHAPTER SIXTEEN

My sisters stayed with me until closing, helping out where they could or chatting with customers as they came in. I think they were just worried about me. Willow kept telling me to stop biting my nails, and Mallory was actually being nice to me.

Margie was letting me come to a photo session she'd already set up with a group of models tomorrow evening on the beach. I was to bring a bathing suit and a dress ... and her doubled fee, of course.

I was a nervous wreck. "What if she takes one look at me and sees I'm a fraud?" I moaned. "Can you be arrested for impersonating a model?"

Frankie shook her head at me with a grin. There was red lipstick on her front teeth. She'd come in with her pups for an update and ended up staying to wait out the brewing black skies and sudden uptick of wind that signaled an impending summer storm. "You could easily pass for a model, sugarplum."

"Yeah, don't worry," Mallory smirked. "Models don't have hips, either."

Well, her being nice to me hadn't lasted long. I threw a dog treat at her and missed.

One of Frankie's pups snatched it up off the floor.

"Too slow, girl." I shrugged at Goldie, who had lifted her head and stared at me to see if I was going to toss another one.

"Just watch the other models and do what they do," Willow said. "You'll be fine. It's not rocket science."

The bell jangled above the door as Charlie pushed through trying to juggle an umbrella and a large bulletin board. A loud clap of thunder boomed and the sky lit up white. We all rushed to help her get inside.

"All of us" included the four dogs, who "helped" by demanding attention from the dripping, laughing Charlie.

"Let her get in the door! Come on." Frankie clapped her hands, calling the dogs away from the chaos.

The excitement of the moment had made them frisky, and they started playing amongst themselves, knocking a row of rubber ball ropes off their hooks in the process.

Goldie grabbed one off the ground and shook it, teasing the other dogs. She soon had three small, jumping fur balls on her heels as she trotted around, playing keep-away.

It warmed my heart to see Goldie having fun. She'd been so depressed when I adopted her.

How would Sandy fit into this group? Would she be annoyed by the antics of the younger dogs? I shook the thought loose. What was I doing? "Okay, Charlie," I said. "Let's get that bulletin board up."

"I got it." Mallory helped Charlie carry the board over to the wall.

Charlie dug a manila envelope out of her tote bag. "Here are some photos to get started, if you want to go through 'em."

As Charlie and Mallory hung the bulletin board on the wall, Frankie, Willow and I looked through the photos.

"You really did a great job on these," Frankie called to her.

"Thanks, I hope it helps." Charlie stepped back to inspect their work. "Does that look straight, guys?"

We all nodded. "Looks great."

I paused on the photo of Sandy. A straw beach hat rested on her head, and her kind eyes stared directly into the camera. She seemed so trusting. She had to be wondering why she'd been abandoned. My heart clenched.

Charlie peered over my shoulder. "I just took that one yesterday. That's the dog you were asking about, right? Sandy? She's sweet. Kinda reminded me of Goldie."

Frankie slid an arm around my shoulder. "You can't save 'em all, sugar."

I swallowed the lump in my throat and nodded. Then took her photo over and tacked it to the middle of the board. I sent up a silent prayer to the universe that she would find a good home soon.

* * *

"So, how'd today go?" I asked Will eagerly as I slid into his sedan. Closing up the boutique had gone much faster with my sisters there to help.

He leaned over and pressed a kiss on my lips. "I don't know yet, my day's not over. I've got a few alibis to follow up on. One right now if you don't mind taking a ride with me over to the Seaboard condos. We can grab a bite after that."

"Sure. Whose alibi are we investigating?"

"Remember the vet tech, Lincoln Lee?"

"Sure."

"Well, he said he'd spent the night with his girlfriend and had a rare Saturday off so they didn't leave her apartment until around noon that day. Thought it'd be better to talk to her in person about verifying that. Seeing as Mr. Lee is tied to both Helping Paws and Southern Cross Clinic and was one of Peter's clients, I don't want to make any mistakes here."

I frowned. "You really think he's capable of murder? He seems so nice."

Will glanced over at me. "Nice people can make bad decisions."

Will rang the apartment doorbell.

When the door opened, I was taken aback. "Daisy?" I blurted out.

Her eyes and smile both widened in surprise. "Darwin! What on God's green earth are you doin' at my door?" She gave me a spontaneous hug.

Her blonde, freshly shampooed curls tickled my nose. Her skin seemed warm and flushed, even though she was wearing a short, sleeveless dress.

When she released me, she glanced at Will. "Oh, forgive me ... Detective Blake, right? Lincoln said to be expecting a call. I didn't realize you'd be calling in person. Well here, I'm being rude, come in, come in." She ushered us inside.

The main space was a living room/dining room combo. The dining room had a glass table centered in a square area of beige tile. The living room had plush cream carpeting and a marble fireplace. There was a cut through to the kitchen and a hallway. The place held the sweet scent of flowers, though I didn't see any in the room.

A white dog with bristly fur pushed itself up and ambled slowly over to us, tail wagging. I bent down, letting him sniff my hand and then took a chance and scratched the brown patch on his chest. No recent trauma, that's good.

"Who's this cutie?" I asked.

"That's Felix. We're still getting to know each other. I just got him from the shelter a few weeks ago. So far, so good, except for a slight skin rash. Lincoln said it might be allergies." She gestured toward a white wicker sofa against the far wall. "He's got the best personality, though. Real chill. Have a seat. Can I get y'all a drink? I have bottled water or sweet tea, my gran's secret recipe."

"No, thank you." Will held up a hand as he perched on edge of the sofa. "We really won't take up much of your time, Miss Beaumont."

I glanced at Will sideways. Some real southern sweet tea would've been nice. But whatever, down to business.

"All right." She slid into a matching chair to our left. "What can I do for you?"

Felix had followed us over to the sofa and now leaned his full weight against my leg. I stroked his head and glanced around the condo.

It was pristine and looked unlived in, like a model home. There was no art on the walls, no nicknacks, no personal touches of any kind. The one exception being a single photo of Daisy and Lincoln sitting on the end table next to me. It looked like it had been taken in some restaurant.

"As you know, I'm investigating the death of Peter Vanek," Will said. "I interviewed Lincoln Lee earlier today, and he said he was with you on the morning of August thirteenth. Can you corroborate that?"

"Well, sure. That Saturday we were together here until around noon. Then we went to lunch at BellaBrava's." Worry pinched her brow. "Detective Blake, you don't really think Lincoln had anything to do with Peter's death do you? I mean, Lincoln was really fond of Peter, as a person and as a photographer. And besides, he's just not that type of guy. He spends his spare time helping animals ... he wouldn't hurt a fly."

Will gave her a disarming smile. "Mr. Vanek was killed with a drug called sux, a very strong muscle relaxant that paralyzes the respiratory muscles. He suffocated, completely aware but unable to move. This drug went missing at the Southern Cross Vet Clinic where Lincoln works so I have to consider everyone who had access to it a suspect. You understand."

Then he let silence fill the room. I could hear a clock ticking nearby. Felix was snoring lightly.

Daisy was staring at Will with her mouth open, her hand around her throat. "Of course. What a horrible way to die."

Will only nodded in agreement. I knew what Will was doing, using the silence as pressure to get her to talk and all that, but I couldn't help myself. I was dying to know something.

"Daisy, you and Lincoln didn't act like you were a couple at Rachel's party. How come?"

She moved her attention to me and shook her head sadly. "Jealousy, plain and simple. Lincoln is one of those rare guys with the whole package—sweet, gorgeous, talented, loyal. He's got more than a few of those models chasin' after him. They will take down any women he dates like a pack of she-wolves, and I just don't want to be in their crosshairs. So I've asked Lincoln to keep our relationship private for now. I'm having a hard enough time getting jobs because of my age, I don't need to add being sabotaged to the list of hurtles."

"How long have you and Mr. Lee been dating?" Will's tone had softened.

"Almost a year." Daisy got that dreamy look in her eye again at the mention of Lincoln. Seemed like she really loved him.

"No wedding bells?" I glanced at her hand. No supersized engagement ring. Lincoln didn't seem like he could afford the type of ring I saw in my vision anyway.

She blushed and smiled softly. "No. We're just enjoying each other's company for now."

Will scribbled something in his notebook then asked, "Have you spent time at Helping Paws Rescue with Lincoln?"

"Well, sure, how do you think I got that little guy?" She nodded down at Felix, who's feet were twitching in his sleep. "You can't go to that place without saving one of 'em. Not if you have a heart."

Guilt twisted my gut and I dropped my eyes.

Was that the universe giving me a nudge? More like a nice, subtle kick in the stomach.

"Did Mr. Lee ever talk to you about the recent controversy surrounding their mobile spay and neuter program?"

She shook her head, a wrinkle appearing between her brows. "I only know what I read in the paper about the fraud accusations. When I asked Lincoln about it, he brushed it off. Said the director's not worried."

"What about any personal conflict with Sassy White? Does he get along with her?"

A wide grin lit up her face. It was dazzling. I could definitely see her in commercials selling toothpaste or those teeth whitening do-hickys. I'd buy 'em.

"Detective, Sassy White has conflict with everyone from what I saw there, but not in a serious way. Lincoln seems to find her amusing. Although ..." Her expression grew thoughtful. "I don't want to spread gossip, but if you're asking about Sassy White in particular ... now that I think about it, I think she may be takin' the fraud investigation more seriously than she's letting on. I did overhear her yelling at somebody in her office a few weeks back ... something about suing the pants off the 'lilly-livered piece of garbage who started the investigation.' Her words, not mine."

"Do you know who was in her office at the time?"

"No, sorry, I was just passing through."

"So you don't know who she was referring to either?"

Daisy shook her head.

"All right. I think that's it for now. Can you spell your last name for me?"

"Sure. You won't find me under Beaumont though, if you're checkin'. That's my stage name. My maiden name is Vanderhall." She spelled it out.

Will scribbled in his notebook and then closed it with a smack. "Well, thank you for your time." He stood and left his business card on the coffee table. "Please give me a call if you think of anything else that might help move the investigation forward."

I patted Felix one last time and then followed Will.

Daisy walked us to the door. "Peter was great, you know. One of the good guys. I hope you find out who did this."

* * *

Will and I grabbed a late supper at The Moon Under Water on the corner of Beach Drive. It had rained recently and water was still dripping off the large red patio umbrella over our table. I pushed my vegetable curry around my plate, too tired to actually chew. I noticed Will had barely touched his burger. Instead, his chin was planted on his fists and his mind was somewhere else as he stared across the street into North Straub Park.

"Maybe we should just box this up and call it a night," I said.

He shook his head, coming back to the moment. "Yeah, sorry. Didn't mean to drift on you."

I signaled for the waitress. "Don't be sorry. We both need some sleep. We'll start fresh in the morning."

Will walked me down the sidewalk, back to the townhouse gate. We turned to each other, and he took my hands in his. I fell forward to rest against his chest, thinking about spending the night there.

He rubbed my neck and kissed the top of my head. "Remember, don't ask Margie Bealle any questions about Vanek tomorrow. You're just trying to get a feel for what type of person she is."

When I didn't respond, he said, "Darwin? Promise me."

I breathed in his slightly salty scent. "Promise," I groaned into his chest. I hoped I could keep that promise.

When I came through the door, Goldie and Petey greeted me like I'd been gone a month. I knelt and wrapped my arms around Goldie, letting her lick my chin. "That's a good girl. I missed you, too."

Petey was jumping and scratching at my leg. I smiled and lifted him up to give him a cuddle, though I knew I should be trying to teach him not to jump up on people. Just because he was knee-high to a grasshopper didn't mean he shouldn't have manners.

"What in the world does Mallory have you dressed in now?" I laughed as I held him out and eyed the blue flannel pajamas covered in hearts.

Willow peered over the kitchen counter. "Hey, Mallory has something she wants to show you. Could be important."

"Besides Petey's new outfit?" One last snuggle and I reluctantly put Petey down. Now I saw why people carry these toy breeds around instead of letting them walk on their own four paws. They were like living stuffed animals.

Both dogs trotted after me into the living room, Petey's little legs moving double time to keep up. I plopped down next to Mallory on the sofa. Lucky was stretched out behind her, so I stroked her tail as I asked, "What's up?"

"Hang on." She clicked the keyboard on her laptop and then turned it to face me. "Check this out. I was going through the photos on the flash drive again and noticed this."

"How do you have the photos?" I asked, surprised.

"I copied them to my computer. That's not the point. Look." She pointed to a black sports car parked next the van and zoomed in.

I glanced from the screen to her skeptically. "A guy sitting in a car?"

"Yeah. Not just a guy though, check this out." She scrolled to the next photo. It was a better angle so I could see the dark-haired man wasn't alone. There was also a blonde woman in the car with him. Mallory scrolled to the next image and zoomed in. They were kissing. Then she quickly moved to the next image. "Here. This is a good shot of her face."

I leaned closer to the screen. She was right, this one was really clear and you could see the blonde's face. She had her mouth open, laughing at something.

"Oh," I said, surprised. "That's Daisy. The dark-haired man must be her boyfriend, Lincoln. Will and I were just at Daisy's apartment tonight." I stared at the image and shrugged. "I don't think this means anything though. They're dating and Lincoln is at the shelter all the time. Nothing out of the ordinary here, no scandal."

Mallory's body sunk deeper into the sofa, like it'd grown heavy. "Shoot. I was hoping it was some politician or something caught red-handed with his mistress."

"No, sorry. Lincoln's just a model and vet tech." A wave of her disappointment washed over me.

Willow came over and handed me a cup of tea. "You need to lay off those romance novels, Mal."

"Very funny," Mallory grumbled.

"Thanks." I gratefully accepted the steaming cup from Willow. Closing my eyes, I inhaled the mango scent. The tension in my muscles released a bit.

We sat silently for a few minutes and tried to think of any reason those photos would be relevant to Peter's case.

We all came up empty.

Mallory closed the laptop with a sigh and turned to me. "Well, since none of us will be able to sleep tonight anyway, Willow and I are going to help you practice. You need to learn the technique Grandma Winters taught us after you left."

Willow chimed in. "She's right, Darwin. Since this woman is coming at us from the water, we feel like you're our best protection."

"I know and I have been practicing," I said defensively.

Willow stared at me in that patient way she had of dealing with the dense and clueless. "And how's it going?"

I squinted at her over the tea cup. "You know how it's going."

"Exactly why you need our help." Willow stood. "Let's go. You'll thank us one day."

I reached down and scooped up Petey, who'd crashed on my foot. "Fine."

Mallory climbed the stairs behind me, cradling Lucky on her shoulder. "You know what Grandma

Winters says, 'You must practice your power until you become the power.'"

I glanced back at her as Goldie pushed past me to get to the bed first. "What does that even mean?"

And what does it mean that Grandma Winters wasn't even our grandmother but instead some guardian sent to make sure we didn't destroy our world?

"You'll understand when it happens," Willow said patiently.

I rolled my eyes. I was too tired for this. Heading to my bedroom first, I tucked Petey into his crate and gave Goldie a good night belly rub as she stretched out on my pillow. "It's all yours tonight, girl."

My sisters were waiting for me in the hall. As I opened the door to my practice room, I had a thought. "Do you think we're actually dangerous?"

Willow nudged me inside. "Any kind of power is dangerous if it's not used with the right intention."

Mallory and I glanced at each other and grinned, repeating the words that had been drummed into us by Grandma Winters since childhood, "The power lies in the intention."

CHAPTER SEVENTEEN

Friday morning I stood at the boutique counter, a bowl of water in front of me. Well, leaned against the counter was more like it. I was truly exhausted. After having a bit of success last night with control, Willow had suggested I try practicing today while dealing with normal daily distractions. It would require more focus. I wasn't sure the frustration levels I was currently feeling were everyday normal, but I was trying anyway.

I closed my eyes and reached out with my mind, searching for the connection with the water, but Mallory's conversation with Patrice Patterson in the nearby fish and bird aisle was the only thing I could focus on. Patrice had the sharp laugh of a parrot. Very distracting. I took a deep breath and blew it out. Petey barked in his fenced area behind me. I startled.

This was not working. I closed my eyes again and the bells jangled on the front door. I opened my eyes.

Sylvia stumbled toward me in sweat pants and dark glasses, her long hair pulled up into a disheveled ponytail.

"Sylvia!" I gasped. The water sloshed out of the bowl, wetting the front of my white sundress. I jumped back.

No control at all. Great.

I raced around the counter and embraced Sylvia in a careful hug. She sniffled on my shoulder as I rubbed her back. "What are you doing here? I mean, it's good to see you and all. But, I thought we agreed it wasn't a good idea for you to be here."

I hoped she wasn't going to make another attempt to work. The dark cloud hanging over her would scare the customers.

She mumbled something in Portuguese and pulled off her sunglasses.

I tried not to react to her swollen eyes and lack of makeup. Sylvia would normally never leave her house without makeup on. Even as bad off as she'd been on Tuesday, she'd still made an effort with some waterproof mascara. Today, *nada*. This was a real bad sign of her deteriorating mental state.

Opening her bag, she dropped her sunglasses in and pulled out a Kleenex. "My mother, my cousins, my aunts ... they are driving me insane." She blew her nose hard. "I had to get away from the negativity."

I took her hand and led her over to the tea table, then stifled a gasp of surprise as she climbed into the chair. *Oh heavens, she was worse off than I thought.* "Um, Sylvia? Do you know you're not wearing shoes?"

She glanced down at her feet and shrugged. "What do shoes matter?"

I cringed and glanced around for help. *What do I do?* I patted her arm. "You stay right here, I'm going to make you some special tea."

I raced into the storage room, pulling out a bottle of emergency flower essence.

Mallory followed me into the storage room. "Where's the fire?"

"Sitting at the tea table. It's Sylvia and she's not wearing shoes." As Mallory's eyes widened, I raced back to Sylvia.

I made the tea and added ten drops of flower essence—and then ten more for good measure. I also tried to calm my mind enough to infuse some calmness into the water.

"Sylvia?" I touched her arm.

She was staring out the window. Slowly, she moved her puffy, red eyes to me, her expression slack.

"Drink this."

She looked down at the cup and took it like she was moving through quicksand.

I stared at her in disbelief as I watched her sip the tea. *Is this what love does to people?*

"Sylvia, listen to me. You are a strong woman, and you're going to get through this no matter what happens. You will survive this."

Her eyes met mine, and I saw at least a flicker of the fire I knew was in there. "I don't want to just survive. I want to have a life with the man I love, with Landon. What is good about just surviving?"

I reached over and squeezed her hand. "Well, have you thought about just marrying him anyway? I mean, plenty of people go against their parents' wishes when they marry someone. It's your life after all."

She smiled sadly. Her head dropped in defeat. "It would kill my mother. Literally. She would die ... heart attack, stroke, whatever ... she physically would not survive me going through with a marriage that she believes is cursed. And she would never forgive me." Sylvia bit her lip hard. Tears welled up in her dark eyes, and her voice cracked as she added, "She would die and then she would haunt me. No. I simply cannot do it."

I wanted to say she didn't know for sure her mother would never forgive her, but she knew her mother best. And if she truly believed that, she'd never take the chance. Back to the original plan. "Okay but we're getting closer to finding Peter's killer, so don't give up hope yet."

Her eyes flicked up to meet mine. "You know it is Friday?" she asked tentatively. "We'd have to have the wedding by Monday if it's going to happen. My family has early flights out Tuesday morning."

"I know." Staring at my devastated friend, I pursed my lips. It was time to take that leap of faith. "You know what, Sylvia? You and Landon just start planning the wedding for Monday evening. Call Frankie. She has your cake and everything stored at the resort. Tell her to start unthawing and unwrapping. She'll help you. Will and I'll have Peter's murderer behind bars by then, I promise." Once the words were out of my mouth, it felt less like a leap of faith and more like a sudden fall to certain death. Too late now. "Do you think you can do that?" I tried to exude more confidence than I felt.

"Well ..." she shook her head and then looked into my eyes. Whatever she saw there must've given her some hope. "Frankie did say she could arrange for us to have the wedding poolside. We would just have to say the word. I told her she was crazy but ... do you really think it's possible?"

My heart melted that Frankie believed in Will and me. "Yes, I do." *Anything is possible, right? Even the impossible.* I slipped her hands in mine and squeezed. "Say the word, Sylvia."

There was still doubt in her eyes, but I could tell she was thinking about it.

The bell over the door jangled. *Oh thank the stars, saved by the bell.*

I smiled at the petite, gray-haired lady who'd entered. "Welcome to Darwin's Pet Boutique, let me know ..." I trailed off as my gaze fell to the dog she'd brought in with her. I slid off the chair. "Is that Felix?"

The woman adjusted her black-framed glasses and smiled up at me. "Yes, I need to get him some grain free food and the Google says you carry it."

Even as I smiled at her charming, accented speech, my mind was reeling. *Did Daisy give Felix away already?* "Sure, follow me."

I took the woman to the food aisle and explained the different brands. Felix seemed to remember me, so I bent down and gave him a good scratch behind the ears.

No trauma. Whatever happened, he was okay with it. *What's going on, boy?*

"I think this one looks good." She pointed to a bag of dry food with a wolf on the front.

"Good choice. Let me get that for you." I hefted the bag onto my shoulder. "Did you need anything else today?"

"Not today, thank you. But I'm sure we'll be back."

As I led them over to the counter, I was explaining how to change Felix's food by mixing a little with his old food at first and then adding more over the next week. But my mind was working on a way to ask her what was going on.

I scanned the barcode on the bag. "So, Felix belongs to Daisy Beaumont right? I just met this little guy recently at her condo."

The woman glanced up at me with an odd expression as she pulled a credit card from her wallet. "Yes, Felix he is Daisy's," she chuckled, "but I wouldn't exactly call her house a condo."

House? Think Darwin.

As the receipt printed out, I squealed. "Oh look at that! You are the one thousandth customer! That means Felix gets a free birthday cake. How lucky are you?" Ignoring her startled expression, I reached beneath the counter and pulled out the cake photo album. "Just pick out one of these delicious cakes for free, and we'll throw in same day delivery."

"Oh, but I don't think it is his birthday." She had her hand on her chest, with the dismayed expression of a woman who was quickly losing control of the situation. Which she was.

I hurried around the counter and opened the book in front of her. "Well, it doesn't have to say happy birthday, we can just write, 'For a lucky dog.' How's that, Felix?" I bent down and let him lick my chin. "He is very excited and I don't blame him. Dogs just love our cakes! They're made with all natural ingredients, too so they're healthy."

Good heavens, I suddenly felt like a used car salesman. It was exhausting. I left her with the book and returned to Sylvia, who was staring at me like I was two crayons short of a box.

"That dog belongs to Daisy Beaumont," I whispered in response to her unasked question. "A lady

Will interviewed yesterday about her boyfriend's involvement..." I suddenly realized it would take too long to explain about the missing sux and the flash drive hidden in Petey's bear and such. And what it all may or may not mean. "You know what ... it's complicated but this may have something to do with Peter's death. I have to see where that dog Felix lives."

She nodded and raised a brow. "You aren't sleeping either are you?"

"No, but..." I waved that off. "I'm fine."

"That's debatable." Mallory came up behind us and, after doing a double-take at Sylvia's appearance, gave her a hug. "Are you going to tell me you're fine, too?"

Sylvia cracked a smile. "No."

"Good, I hate liars." Mallory grinned and turned to me. "What's up with the free cake?"

"Just hold down the boutique for a bit, okay? That little dog there is Felix, and he belongs to Daisy Beaumont, the blonde in the car photos. Something's up and I have to go see what."

"Car photos?" Sylvia asked.

I glanced at Mallory. "Can you fill her in? I've got to get back over there."

"Sure."

I stood beside the woman. "So, have we decided?"

She nodded and pointed at the bone-shaped one. "I guess that one's fine. Thank you." For someone getting a free cake, she sure seemed suspicious of my motives. Or maybe I was just projecting.

"Great!" I pulled out an order form. "Just fill in the name and address and sign there, and we'll get that to you later this afternoon."

After the woman left I took the form over to Mallory and Sylvia, who had some color back in her face at least.

I pointed to the address on the form. "That's one of those historic waterfront mansions on Snell Island, isn't it?"

Sylvia stared at the address and nodded. "Snell Harbor Drive....*si*. Very expensive homes."

Could Daisy possibly live in one of these homes and not in the condo?

"Well, guess I better go see a cake about getting baked … or an oven about baking a cake … however the saying goes. I need to get my butt in gear and go bake a cake."

CHAPTER EIGHTEEN

Two hours later, with the cake still warm, I pulled my VW Beetle around the brick circle drive and parked in front of the Snell Island two-story Mediterranean mansion.

A large oak tree, strung with white lights, stood proudly in the front yard along with a giant, white-marble lion statue. The stucco exterior was a warm tangerine color with bright white trim. A rod iron railing ran along both the first and second story porches, then curved in two c-shapes along the front steps.

I had the convertible top down, and the scents coming from all the flowering plants in the immaculate landscaping were intoxicating. No time to stop and smell the roses, though. I was a girl on a mission for the truth.

Making my way up the steps, I peered through the leaded glass double doors as I waited for someone to answer the doorbell. The first sign of life was Felix, wagging his tail as he traversed the expansive white-marble tiled hallway toward me. I waved at him.

As he reached the door, the lady who'd brought him into the pet boutique appeared from the right, wiping her hands on a dishtowel. She smiled at me through the glass and then opened the door. Her gray bangs were damp and sticking to her forehead and her face was flushed. She was obviously in the middle of something.

Felix got busy sniffing my toes.

"That was fast," she said, reaching for the cake. "Thank you."

Shoot, I needed to get into the house.

I handed it over reluctantly. "Um, I don't mean to be a pest but would it be possible to use your powder room?" I did a little wiggle to show it was an emergency.

"Oh." She glanced behind her. "I suppose." She opened the door wider and I slid in.

Success!

"This way." She led me down the large, echoing hallway, past a formal dining room and to a guest powder room.

"Thanks a bunch." I smiled, hoping I looked more innocent than I felt at the moment.

Felix had followed on our heels, and he had his nose tilted up, trying to sniff the cake.

The woman chuckled. "I think I better go put this on the kitchen counter, out of reach."

"Good idea." I leaned down and gave Felix a scratch. "Don't worry about me. I can see you're busy so I can find my way out. Hope you enjoy the cake, Felix."

I pretended to close the door, but once she'd gone, I pushed it opened and slipped back out. I needed to find some evidence that Daisy actually lived here and not in the condo we'd visited.

Moving quietly, I went the opposite way from the front door.

On the left was a formal living room with dark wood floors and rich, chocolate leather furniture. I walked in. It smelled like furniture polish and faintly of cigar smoke. Glancing around, I spotted photos on the fireplace mantle. Moving quickly across the room to scan them, I zeroed in on one of the 8x10's.

Bingo! There was Daisy.

She was wearing a formal but feminine black suit, her hair pulled back into a severe bun. She was seated in a chair and an older gentleman was hunched behind her, one hand on the back of her chair and one hand on a cane. He also wore a black suit.

My heart sank. I understood now. This was her father's house ... or maybe even her grandfather's? The guy looked pretty old. She probably stayed here part time to take care of him. No scandal there.

Sighing, I turned around to leave and then froze.

Daisy stood in the doorway in a pink, fitted dress, her arms folded, a confused expression on her face.

"Daisy!" I squeaked. "Hi."

"Darwin? What on God's green earth are you doing here?"

I moved closer to her, my smile frozen on my face. Getting caught snooping in someone's house had to be the lowest form of humiliation. I was beyond mortified. "I'm so sorry. I took a wrong turn exiting the bathroom ..."

Then I remembered she wouldn't even know why I was in the bathroom. "Oh, did your ... the woman who brought Felix in my pet boutique today for some gluten free food ... did she tell you she won a free cake? So I delivered it today is why I'm here. In your living room. Well, actually I had to use the ladies' room is why I'm in your living room, but the cake is why I'm in your house." I squeezed my lips together. I wanted to slink past her and run to the car. That wouldn't be socially acceptable though, I'm sure. Instead I waited for her to respond.

Finally, her eyes flicked from me to the fireplace photos. She grew subdued. "Do you recognize Peter's work?"

I glanced behind me, confused for a moment, and then it hit me. "Oh, the photos of you and your father? Peter took those?"

Her gaze moved abruptly back to my face, and the sweet smile I'd come to associate with her resurfaced. "Yes, in his studio. We just had those taken last month for his birthday. We use ... used him for all our family portraits."

"They're very good." I didn't know what else to say, and I was suddenly speechless as I stared at her hand. On her left ring finger sat the engagement ring I'd seen in my vision from Petey. My mouth went dry. My heart did a somersault in my chest.

When I met her eyes again, she was still smiling but they were sharper. *Or was that my imagination?*

I motioned to her hand and forced words from my constricted lungs. "Did you and Lincoln get ... engaged?"

She glanced down and then suddenly broke out in a girlish giggle. It was pleasant, which confused me in my state of anxiety. "No, no." She lifted her hand and examined it. "This is just a family heirloom. I like to wear it around the house when I'm not out in public. No sense inviting a mugging. Lovely, isn't it?" She held it out for me to examine. "Almost six carats set in platinum. The side stones are rubies and sapphires."

I felt the tension drain from my body as I crossed the room to get a closer look.

Yep, definitely the ring. Wow, her family must be loaded.

"It's stunning. Very unique." Something was wriggling around in my gut still.

What was it? Oh yeah. My vision. Why would Daisy be putting Petey in his carrier? I really needed to think about what that meant.

"Well, I need to get back to the pet boutique. It was good to see you again. Hope Felix enjoys his cake."

"Of course, I'll walk you out."

When we got to the door, Felix trotted around the corner licking his lips.

Smiling, I gave him a pat goodbye. Then I had an idea. "You know, I'm fostering Peter's Yorkie pup until I can find him a home. You wouldn't be interested in a little brother for Felix would you?"

She crossed her arms and grinned at me good-naturedly. "Nice try. Peter already tried to get me to take that puppy home when we were there getting our portraits made. I would've loved to, honestly. He's a precious little thing. But for one, my father can't see very well and accidently stepped on him at the studio. I felt terrible. Also, I don't know the first thing about puppies and potty trainin'. Felix here is easy, already trained."

"Yeah," I agreed. "Puppies are a lot of work and he is very tiny. All right, see ya around."

I pulled back onto 20th Avenue feeling disap-pointed. There was a logical explanation for both the house and Daisy being the one to put Petey in his crate in my vision. Obviously she had put Petey in his crate to be safe after her father accidently stepped on him. Being stepped on was a bit traumatic for the little guy so my vision had nothing to do with Peter's death.

Back to square one. I needed to talk to Will and see if he'd come up with anything this morning. Time was definitely running out now. And I'd gone and promised Sylvia a wedding.

A wave of frustration overwhelmed me. I banged my head against the steering wheel at the light. "Way to go, Darwin."

* * *

Will and I met for lunch at Parkshore Grill. It wasn't the pleasant affair it usually was, though, since both of us were slumped in the booth lost in our own thoughts. Twirling my straw in my ice water, I finally sighed and broke the silence. "I was so sure once we'd found the owner of that engagement ring from my vision, we'd have the murderer."

Did I just say that out loud?

I glanced up in time to see discomfort darken Will's expression.

He quickly hid it and reached across the table to take my hand. "Don't be hard on yourself, Darwin. It's me who's failing here. I'm the one who should be coming up with the hard facts to solve this."

Hard facts, right. Not visions. They weren't useful. Message received.

I tamped down my hurt, and was just about to change the subject, when I caught sight of someone out of the corner of my eye. Zach was standing outside the window on the sidewalk. I met his gaze through the glass. He held up a hand in greeting. A small smile stretched on my lips as I waved back.

Then I felt the emptiness as Will's hand left mine. I glanced at Will. He was staring at Zach, his expression unreadable.

Zach's gaze moved from me to Will, then he nodded and walked away.

Well, that was awkward.

"What's the deal with that guy, anyway?" Will asked without actually looking at me.

"What do you mean?" I knew what he meant and felt my face growing hot at the question. Will wasn't stupid. In fact, he was probably the most observant person I knew, and it didn't take a very observant person to recognize the way Zach looked at me.

"Never mind, we have enough to worry about." He leaned back as the waitress placed two steaming plates of pasta in front of us. When she left, he said, "Let's talk this out one more time. I think one of our most important pieces of evidence here is that vial of missing sux from the Southern Cross clinic."

"But it went missing *after* Peter's death," I reminded him, silently grateful for the change of subject.

"Still, too much of a coincidence that it went missing from the very vet clinic connected with Helping Paws, where Peter spent a lot of time volunteering, and where he took the photos he hid on the thumb drive." He shoved a forkful of warm pasta in his mouth and chewed thoughtfully. After he swallowed he added, "And those photos would be the second important piece of evidence."

I nodded. "It does make the most sense. That someone stole his cameras and laptop looking for those photos."

Will pointed his fork at me. "But why were they so important to the killer? Was it the time-stamped van photos which were the obvious subject? Or was it the accidentally captured photos of Lincoln Lee and Daisy Beaumont?"

I shifted in the booth, feeling the weight of the question. Seemed to be the million-dollar one. "Well, if it was the van photos, then Sassy would be the most likely suspect."

Will nodded. "If they would prove she was committing fraud, yes."

"But if it was the photos of Lincoln and Daisy the killer was after, then one of them would be the most likely suspect."

Will pushed aside his plate half-eaten. "Only if they knew about the photos, though. How would they know Vanek had them?"

I followed his line of thought. "They'd only know if Peter told them he had them. And he'd have no reason to tell them unless he was using the photos against them. Blackmailing them for some reason. Maybe that's where the money for his shelter was coming from."

Will's attention went to the window for a moment and then he shook his head. "Lincoln Lee is a struggling model and vet tech. I don't think he has that kind of money. And Ms. Beaumont's not exactly had a successful modeling career."

I held up a finger, getting that rush of adrenaline that happened when I felt something clicking but couldn't quite see it yet. "But Daisy's family does. Her father's house is one of those multi-million dollar mansions in the historic district. If Peter was blackmailing them, maybe she was planning on getting the money from her father."

Will sat completely still, but the intensity of his thoughts blazed in his blue eyes. After a moment he said, "But we're still missing motive in that theory. Why would Ms. Beaumont care if there were photos of her and Lincoln Lee together? Sure, she said she didn't want to be hassled by the other models if they found out, but succumbing to blackmail and committing murder to hide the fact they're dating? Doesn't add up."

I gazed out the window, trying to force my brain to put something together that made sense. Who *would* care that much that Daisy and Lincoln were dating?

I watched a family of four walk by with ice cream cones. An overweight chocolate lab with them stared up hopefully for drippings. I turned back to Will. "It's a long shot but what if her father wouldn't have approved of the relationship for some reason? What if she was hiding it from him?"

A sadness rode in on a small wave. It took a moment for me to root out the cause. *Oh, yeah.* The realization that I would've loved for my father to meet Will. I'm sure he would've approved. But even if it was possible for him to be here, would Will accept him?

Will reached across the table and laid a warm hand over mine. "You okay?"

I nodded, giving him a half smile. Those observation skills again. "Fine. I was just thinking about how I would've liked my father to meet you."

Will smiled and rubbed the amethyst promise ring he'd given me. "I would've liked my parents to meet you, too. They would've loved you as much as I do." He glanced up. "What about your mom? I'd really like to meet her."

"Oh." A lump formed in my throat. "I'm not exactly her favorite daughter right now. She still hasn't forgiven me for leaving Savannah."

"I'm sorry," Will said. "Maybe in time then."

"Yeah, sure. In time." I nodded and blinked back tears.

Will noticed and changed the subject. "Okay. I guess it's worth a call to Ms. Beaumont's father and, if nothing else, rule out that theory. If he knows about his daughter's relationship with Mr. Lee and isn't vehemently against it, then I'll have to switch directions and really bear down on Sassy White later today. Bring her into interrogation. It's early and I've really got nothing on her, but if I show her the van photos Vanek took maybe it'll provoke an emotional response. Maybe even cause her to slip up and confess."

I leaned back into the soft back of the booth. "Does that really work?"

Will looked tired suddenly. "You'd be surprised what people will confess to if they feel guilty enough." He glanced out the window and shook his head. "I can't shake the feeling that we're missing something around the money, though." He scrubbed a hand roughly over his face. "We ran a check on the people who donated to Vanek's Fund-Me page. There was one lady who is wealthy. A Bianca Rubio. She gave five hundred dollars but according to my team, she's a hotel heiress worth a few million. She could've been a blackmail target, but over what? I have no idea. We're planning on interviewing her, though. At least find out what her relationship with Vanek was."

"Sounds like a plan." I asked for a box when the waitress returned and we prepared to leave. "I was supposed to go to that group photo shoot tonight on the beach with Margie Bealle. Do you think I should cancel? Seems less likely she's involved."

Especially now that I've already discovered the owner of the large engagement ring from my vision.

Will slid out of the booth and then held out his hand to help me. "You should still go. See what the models know about Daisy and Lincoln's relationship, if anything."

CHAPTER NINETEEN

Even if Margie Bealle hadn't have given me the colorful South Beach hotel on Treasure Island as a landmark, I would've been able to find the photo shoot. All I had to do was follow the flock of men who'd migrated from the Friday night drum circle further down the beach.

"Great. An audience," I mumbled, trudging across the sun-warmed, packed-down white sand. I tugged at the small bikini top I'd borrowed from Mallory, wishing I'd thrown on a robe instead of just a pair of shorts.

This idea was going from bad to worse.

A group of black beaked shorebirds scurried toward the edge of the water as I approached. I spotted Margie Bealle talking to a tall blonde in a shiny gold bikini at the water's edge.

Margie was a stocky woman. Her short, dark hair was held back with a purple bandana, and a camera was slung around her neck. Four other bikini-clad women stood around, their various shades of long hair blowing in the ocean breeze. Two of them I recognized from Rachel's party. One, the red-head, looked familiar, but I couldn't remember where I'd seen her before. They were too busy touching up makeup and adjusting various body parts to notice me, thank heavens.

Two men were also standing around equipment bags in the sand. One of them was busy propping up a large metallic panel of some kind. They also paid no attention to me. They were too entranced by the real models.

"Margie." I plastered on a smile as I approached. "Hi, I'm Darwin Winters. Thank you so much for squeezing me in." I purposely didn't look at the woman she was standing with. Rude, I know, but my courage was on shaky ground to begin with.

Margie gave me the once over, then reached out and took my chin in her hand. "I hope you brought some concealer for those dark circles under your eyes."

Makeup. Right. Well, that only took what ... three seconds for my ignorance of this foreign world to show itself. "Oh, I'm sorry ... I forgot."

I felt a hand on my arm. "I have some you can borrow. Come on."

The model I'd been terrified to look at was suddenly my savior, and I told her so ... repeatedly.

"All right, ladies." Margie clapped her hands. "The warm lighting is happening. Let's get this show on the road. Tisha, you're up."

I accepted the mirror and stick of makeup. "Thanks."

"No problem. I'm Cindy, by the way. This your first time working with Margie?"

I tapped the cream in beneath my eye and smoothed it in. *Huh, what do you know, it actually worked.* "Yeah. I used to use Peter Vanek ... before ... you know, he died."

She nodded. "Such a shame. He was a good guy. I used him when I started out last year, but he was always so overbooked. Margie's all right. You just have to ignore her temper. It's not personal."

"Temper?" I handed her back the concealer stick.

Cindy shrugged. "She's passionate about her art."

"Cindy! Get your butt over here!" Margie yelled from the shoreline.

Cindy grinned. "See what I mean? You'll be fine." She swiveled and jogged down to the water on the balls of her feet. It was like a scene out of Baywatch and elicited a few whistles from the crowd.

Margie shot them a look and they stopped.

I walked down to watch Cindy's photo shoot, hoping to grab some tips for my turn.

Cindy moved smoothly, standing at first, tilting her chin one way and then the other. Her expression morphed from pure joy to sultry sex kitten. *Yeah, that wasn't happening for me.* She kneeled down and let the soft waves rush over her thighs.

"Stick that chest out, Cindy! Beach Body Magazine doesn't want some hunched over animal on their cover!"

I backed up a step and accidently stepped on someone's foot. "Sorry!" I gasped.

"No worries. I've got another one," the model behind me laughed easily. "You seem nervous. First time?"

I deflated. "That obvious, huh?"

She gave my arm a squeeze. "You'll be fine. Just ignore everyone and have fun."

"Just have fun. I'll try. Thanks." Glancing over my shoulder, I noticed the men were all taking photos with camera phones. I fought the urge to flee.

"Darwin! You're up."

Too late.

I felt my body obeying her. My feet shuffled through the sand toward the water and probable humiliation.

"Let's go, move it!" she yelled. "This light won't last forever."

When my toes hit the water, I felt my body relax. I wasn't worried about the psycho mermaid here—too many witnesses. So I let myself go, connecting with the water and feeding on that connection for strength and courage.

As I turned and faced the camera, I tilted one hip down and lowered my chin like I'd seen Cindy do. A burst of flash from the camera encouraged me.

"Good. Throw a hand on your hip."

The young, silent guy with the gold panel moved to my right and held it up a few feet from me.

Did he mean to blind me? *Don't squint.* I placed a hand on my right hip as Margie had asked. *Now what?* I tried to change my facial expression from a smile to something sultrier.

"More sexy, less confused!" Margie barked.

Just then, I tripped over my own foot and landed in the water. A collective "oooo" came from the crowd.

Smooth, Darwin. I tried to play it off and threw my hand on my other hip, smiling again.

Margie was shaking her head. "All right, Grace … while you're down there let's get you up on all fours. I got some nice backlighting on that platinum hair of yours."

When it was over, I plopped down in the sand wearing Mallory's little black dress and watched the other girls finish up. I felt like I'd just been sideswiped and was trying to get my bearings. The other girls made it look so easy and none of them looked as emotionally wiped out as I now felt.

Cindy stood over me, sliding a slinky silver dress over her bikini. "Hey, we're heading over to party at Suite Six. You should come."

I pushed myself up and dusted sand off the dress. Spending time in a noisy club with a group of twenty-somethings wasn't my idea of a good time. I just wanted to go home to my sisters, dog and a hot bath to scrub off the humiliation. But, it would give me a chance to ask everyone what they knew about Lincoln and Daisy so I reluctantly agreed. "Sure. Just give me a sec."

"Hey," I said to Margie as she was packing up. "Thanks again for squeezing me in." I was trying to think of some way to bring up Peter and coming up empty.

"Yeah, sure." She stood and hefted her large black camera bag over a shoulder. "Piece of advice?"

I nodded. "Of course."

She shook her head slightly and then patted me on the shoulder. "Don't quit your day job, Kid."

* * *

Walking into the club with five models felt like we were playing a game of "one of these things is not like the other." It was the most self-conscious I've ever felt, especially after Margie Bealle's parting advice. I swear a spotlight flicked on and the music came to a screeching halt as everyone turned to stare at us. I'm hoping that all happened in my head. Hard to tell.

By the time we got to the bar, there was already a gaggle of men waiting to buy us drinks. I tried to order water, but a tequila shot was shoved into my hand ... repeatedly. After the whirlwind shot-fest, Cindy pulled me out onto the dance floor. The music pounded through my body, making it feel like my heartbeat was outside myself. We were immediately engulfed in a sea of bodies, jerking and pulsing to the beat.

"Loosen up!" Cindy yelled in my ear, laughing. Her breath smelled like tequila.

I nodded and tried to imitate her hip movements. Mallory was wrong, some models do have hips.

Someone's hands came from behind and rested on my own hip bones. Then a sweaty body pressed into me.

Startled, I whirled around.

Just a random guy. I backed up a little out of his reach and bumped into another body. Claustrophobia was setting in.

Through the crowd, there was one still figure on the edge of the dancing horde. *Zach. How in the world did he always know where I was?* I pushed my way through the hot, sweaty, pulsating mass of bodies, but by the time I broke free he was gone.

Sighing, I forced my way through the smaller crowd at the bar and ordered a soda water with lime, then went to search for the other girls. I found three of them at a tall, round table, surrounded by hopeful suitors. I'd seen the same look on Goldie's face when I pulled freshly baked treats out of the oven.

I slid next to Malaika, the girl Daisy had introduced me to at Rachel's party. "Great place. Having fun?"

She sipped a glass of champagne and shrugged. "A bit crowded and loud for my tastes."

Good, the guys were buffering the dance music enough that we could hear each other.

"Hey, you know Lincoln? That cute model that was at Rachel's party?"

Her head was bobbing to the music. "Yeah?"

"Is he dating anyone that you know of?"

She shook her head and smirked. "No, but you're barkin' up the wrong tree. He's turned everyone one of us down so we figure he must be gay."

"Too bad." I feigned disappointment.

Glancing around the table, I reached out my hand to the redhead, who was holding her hair up in a sweaty pile on top her head. "Hey, I'm Darwin."

She shook my hand firmly. "Bianca." Her translucent skin was flushed and her light green eyes were glassy.

Bianca?

And then it hit me. Where I'd seen her before. She was the redhead in the photo on Peter's dresser. "Sorry," I said, realizing she was trying to pull her hand away. I moved around Malaika and squeezed in between her and Bianca. "Bianca Rubio?"

She nodded and downed the rest of whatever was in her glass.

A short man in a sweaty black button-down shirt took the opportunity to grab her glass. "What's your pleasure, love?"

She glanced over at him, distracted. "I'm leaving. Thanks anyway."

"Right. Next time maybe?"

When she didn't answer, he got the hint and sulked off.

"That must get annoying," I said, trying to start the conversation up again.

"Only when they don't take the hint, and I have to get rude." She opened her tiny black bag on the table and took out Chapstick. After applying it generously to her peach-colored lips, she turned to me. "So, who're you with?"

I smiled. This time I knew what the question meant. "No one. I'm just starting out, actually. Trying to build up my portfolio. I wanted to use Peter Vanek. I heard such great things about him. But ... you know. Such a tragedy. Did you know him?"

Her green eyes glittered as she stared at me. A strong wave of emotion rushed through me like dry heat. I couldn't tell what it was. Fear? Grief? Anger? "No. I didn't." Her mouth moved a bit more and then clamped shut. She scooped her tiny bag off the table. "Gotta run. Night, girls."

She pushed away from the table. The crowd swallowed her, and she was gone.

I turned to Malaika. "Was it something I said?"

She patted my hand sympathetically. "She was in love with Peter."

CHAPTER TWENTY

Saturday morning, I dragged my weary soul downstairs to open the pet boutique. It was so quiet in the empty space, just me and Goldie. I really missed Sylvia and her loud, happy enthusiasm for life.

As I flipped the open sign around, I glanced down at Goldie. She was watching out the door expectantly, her tail a flag swooshing back and forth. Could she be missing Sylvia, too?

"Don't worry, girl. When she comes back, she'll be Mrs. Sylvia Stark. Things will work out. They have to."

Goldie looked up at me—maybe a little skeptically, or I could've been projecting—and then went to lay beneath the tea table where she could stare out the window.

An hour later, Mallory walked through the door behind a well-dressed elderly couple and their two miniature gray poodles. I didn't recognize the couple so I spent a moment showing them around the boutique. When I was done, I found Mallory at the tea table.

She eyed me with a slight grin. Her green eyes were alight with humor. "Someone got in late last night."

"Yeah, I'm definitely too old for the antics of twenty-something models." Sighing, I took Petey from her and snuggled my nose into his neck. I got my ear chewed on with baby vampire teeth for the effort, but I didn't care. Nothing like puppy breath to relieve stress.

She chuckled. "How'd the shoot go?"

"As good as I thought it would, and I don't ever want to talk about it. The photos will be burned when I get them." I slid in the seat next to her. "But I went out dancing with the girls afterwards and I learned one of the models that was there, Bianca Rubio, was in love with Peter. But, that's not her only connection. Will checked her out after seeing her name on the Fund-Me page Peter had set up, said she's a hotel heiress worth a couple million. That windfall of cash he was expecting … it could've been coming from her. I left a message for Will last night. Hopefully he'll get her in for an interview today."

I glanced around to make sure no customers were near enough to overhear our conversation. No use getting a reputation as a gossip. "Also, I didn't get a chance to tell you … it turns out it's Daisy's father who owns the Snell Island house, so she has a legit reason to be there. No scandal or motive, unless her father doesn't approve of her relationship with Lincoln … but even that seems a thin motive for murder. Will's gonna have a chat with him today anyway and if nothing pans out there, he's gonna bring Sassy White into the station for some questioning. He'll show her the time-stamped photos Peter took of her mobile spay van. See if that gets her riled up enough to talk."

Frowning, Mallory scooped Petey back out of my arms and adjusted the blue "mama's boy" t-shirt she'd dressed him in. "Sounds like Will's got his work cut out for him today. I can't believe you promised Sylvia y'all will have this all figured out by Monday. She actually looked a bit hopeful when she left, thanks to you." Her expression was half admonishment and half pity.

I cringed inwardly. "I know. Not the smartest thing for me to say. I just hope Grandma Winters was right when she said the universe conspires to help us. We need all the help we can get."

Mallory seemed to soften. "Well, she usually is right." She reached out and gave me an uncharacteristic hug. "All right, I'll take the dogs for a potty break. You deal with Mr. Ostermeyer." She jerked her head toward the man who was slowly shuffling toward the counter and whispered, "Last time he was in, he kept calling me Dottie and tryin' to hug me. And he smells like mothballs."

I gave her a chastising half-smile. "That was his wife's name. He's harmless, just a little dementia. Go on. I've got him." I clipped Goldie's leash on for Mallory, gave my dog some vigorous scratches under her ears and then added, "And stop carryin' Petey around everywhere, you're spoiling him rotten."

She snatched Goldie's leash from me. "Whatever. That's what these tiny dogs are good at. Being spoiled."

Frankie came through the door a few minutes after Mallory left. I was just ringing Mr. Ostermeyer up for five cans of cat food. Unfortunately, his cat Precious was no longer with him, but in his less senile moments it made him happy to believe she was. *Who was I to take that away from him?*

I handed him his bag. "You take care of yourself and Precious now, Mr. Ostermeyer. It's hotter than the devil's armpit out there."

"You always did worry too much, Dottie." Reaching a wobbly hand across the counter, he squeezed my hand. Then he smiled a toothless smile. "I've made it this far."

"You sure have." I looked over at Frankie with a grin after he left. "I think he forgot his teeth today."

She chuckled. "Could be worse. Could'a been his pants." She motioned me over to the table. "So, come fill me in. What's goin' on with the investigation? I got a call from Sylvia giving me the okay to plan the wedding for Monday night?" Her eyebrows shot up. Her eyes sparkled with both amusement and worry.

I groaned and plopped down on the chair across from her. "I might've promised her that Will and I would serve up Peter's murderer by then."

She stared at me like I might need a padded room. "Hope can be a dangerous thing, Darwin. Especially for someone in the shape she's in. And Landon's not much better off, let me tell you. I ran into him in Publix yesterday. He was just standing there in the frozen section, starin' at a bag of peas in his hand."

Well, that made me feel like dirt. I shoved my hands into my hair, the panic quickening my heartbeat. "Oh good heavens, Frankie. What have I done? This is such a mess. What if we can't do it? What if she gets this wedding planned ... once again ... and it falls apart ... once again. That seems like too much for anyone to bear. And this time it'll be my fault for making a promise I couldn't keep."

Frankie patted my arm. "I wish I could give you an answer, Darwin. Sometimes things just don't work out the way we want 'em to. That's life."

I felt the tears prick my eyes. Picking up a napkin, I dabbed beneath them to try and stop the overflow.

"Oh, sugar." Frankie folded her hands and scooted forward on the chair. "All right, tell me what you've got so far, maybe having someone with a fresh perspective will help see some connection you and Will have missed."

Nodding thankfully, I summarized all the information we knew so far for her and brought her up to speed on the thumb drive found in Petey's bear.

What else? "Oh yeah, also in the background of those photos, there's a couple getting cozy in the front seat of a black sports car. The guy's a vet tech from Southern Cross Clinic, the vet's office where the sux went missing. His name is Lincoln and the girl's his girlfriend, Daisy. It's possible they're involved somehow. But, we've talked to both of them and can't find any reason they'd be upset Peter had photos of them together."

"So neither of them is a public figure or married?" Frankie asked.

I shook my head. "Nope. The only person we can come up with who they could possibly be hiding from is Daisy's father. Maybe he wouldn't have approved of Lincoln for some reason. Plus, he's got money so if Peter was blackmailing them with the photos, it's possible Daisy was planning on getting the money from her father somehow. Obviously, she couldn't tell him what it was for. I don't know … seems like we're reaching for straws. But what else can we do? Anyway, Will's going to talk to Daisy's father today and see if he knows about her relationship with Lincoln."

Frankie pursed her lips and frowned. "What makes Will think Daisy's father wouldn't approve? Is Lincoln some kind of derelict?"

"No, not at all. Everyone seems to think he's a stand-up guy, and he seems sweet as pie. But when you consider the fact that Peter might've been using those photos to blackmail somebody—and that's where his windfall of cash was coming from—there's only two possibilities. Either he's blackmailing Sassy White with the time-stamped van photos or he's blackmailing Daisy and Lincoln. Seems Daisy's father is the only person in the equation with the kind of money worthy of blackmail. He's got that big pink mansion on the Coffeepot Bayou with the huge live oak out front."

Well, there was Bianca, too. But, she had nothing to do with the photos on the thumb drive, and that had to be connected to all this somehow.

Frankie tilted her head, her eyes narrowing. "The house with that monstrous lion statue in the front yard?"

I nodded. "Yeah, that's the one."

She shook her head slowly, her expression registering confusion. "But that's Barron Vanderhall's place."

"Yes. Vanderhall is Daisy's maiden name. He's her father."

Her eyes widened, mascara-heavy lashes touching her penciled-on brows. "Wait, you're talking about that Daisy? Pretty blonde about thirty?"

"Yes?"

"Oh Darwin." Her hand went to her mouth as she shook her head slowly. "Barron isn't her father."

CHAPTER TWENTY-ONE

I hated to leave Mallory to close up the boutique without me, especially with the crazy mermaid woman stalking us. But Willow'd agreed to come down and stay with her. Besides, this was an emergency. Will wasn't answering his phone, and now I was worried about him, too.

I glanced over at Goldie, who was buckled in the passenger seat of my Beetle convertible. The top was down, her ears were blowing in the breeze, and she was blissfully unaware of all the human drama going on. I probably should've left her with my sisters, but I didn't feel like being alone right now. As I crossed the Snell Isle Bridge and rolled up to the stop sign, I groaned and rested a hand on her.

"What if he's gone over to Daisy's and found out what Frankie just told me? What if he confronted her? And now he's layin' on her marble floor just like Peter?"

Goldie's head swiveled at the sound of my voice. She licked my bare shoulder. A bit of slobber, carried by the breeze, hit the side of my face. I wiped it absentmindedly with the back of my hand.

"You're right. Will is a trained detective. He's smart and completely capable of dealing with whatever happens." Still, he's going into a situation with the wrong information.

I mashed the gas pedal. I couldn't believe she lied right to my face like that. "My father can't see very well," I imitated her, getting more and more angry.

If she'd lied about that what else was she lying about? I was now questioning everything she'd ever told me. Why did she really put Petey in his travel bag? And when? Maybe that vision did happen on the morning of Peter's death.

I crawled down the tranquil, red bricked street; rolling past gated fences and giant mature oak and palm trees shadowing the manicured lawns. Braking, I parked between Daisy's house and her neighbor's— beneath the shade of an oak tree—hoping I wouldn't be spotted by either party. I shut off the car.

Goldie watched me expectantly as I unbuckled her.

The street was quiet. Eerily quiet. Like the calm before the storm.

"I know," I whispered. "Now what?" I stroked Goldie's head and stared at the empty driveway. "Well, Will's car isn't here. That's a good sign, right?"

Saliva from her tongue dripped onto my bare leg. I didn't bother to wipe it off. More important fish to fry.

I tried Will's phone again. Right to voicemail. I hadn't really thought this through. I couldn't just show up on Daisy's doorstep again. Will would not appreciate me confronting her on my own and frankly, I wasn't sure what the woman was capable of. Obviously, I didn't know her at all.

My leg shook as I wracked my brain for a reason to knock on her door. I needed to at least see if Will had been there already and if he had, make sure he had left unharmed.

A sudden low growl started in Goldie's throat. My heart jumped. I followed her attention to the space between the side yards, where the blue water of the bayou sparkled at the edge of their manicured lawns.

I froze. There staring back at us was the crazy woman, still as a statue, standing out in the open for anyone to see. And she wasn't alone. A large wolf-like creature bristled beside her.

My mind flashed back to the first dream I'd had about my father. They were both there. The fish-woman and the wolf.

How could I forget that? My body started trembling uncontrollably.

And then the wolf moved. Like lightning. It bolted through the yard straight for us.

Instinctively, I slid lower in the seat. There was nowhere to go. I was too terrified to control my water magick and had too little time anyway. Before I could suck in a breath, the beast was standing in the road, his eyes locked on us.

The hair on my arms stood up as I stared in disbelief over the curve of my hood.

This can't be happening. But it was. I could smell the musky scent of wild animal mixed with stale, fishy brine water.

Its lips were curled back from impressively long teeth. Saliva hung in strings, connecting its mouth with the road beneath massive paws. Eyes glowed as they locked onto Goldie.

I screamed. I know I did, but no sound reached my ears as, with one last sharp bark, Goldie leaped from the car.

No. No. No! "Goldie!" Her name squeezed through my constricted throat, useless. I fumbled for the door handle as my brave girl began to circle the wild animal, her own teeth bared. She looked like a stuffed animal compared to the massive wolf. She didn't stand a chance. I'd forgotten about the woman. My single thought was to get between Goldie and the wolf.

On one rubber leg I stepped out of the car. I could hear nothing but my own ragged breath and impossibly loud heartbeat.

And then suddenly there was a third animal. A large black dog, almost matching the size of the wolf, poised between Goldie and the beast. Its legs were spread wide, its head lowered with a menacing red glare. The hair stood up on its back in a line from head to tail.

Zach! I'd never been so happy to see him in my life.

"Goldie!" I managed to get the scream out this time. She turned to me, her head and tail high. "Come!"

I watched as she glanced back at the two massive canines, circling, closing in on each other. Thankfully, she bolted to me. I wrapped my arms around her. She was shaking. Or was that me? "Shhh ... it's okay. Such a brave girl."

I suddenly remembered the woman. Twisting my body around from the kneeling position, I peered up over the car and squealed. She was moving toward us, calmly, like she had all the time in the world. "Goldie, come!"

Leaping up, I cut across Daisy's yard, past the giant lion statue and up the driveway with Goldie at my heels. I was definitely going to have a heart attack. I could feel the woman behind me. I knew she was closing in effortlessly. I couldn't bring myself to look back.

My feet pounded up the steps, my gaze locked on the front door.

Okay universe, this is your chance. Help us please! I closed my eyes as I reached for the door handle and willed it to open.

Someone felt sorry for me because miraculously, it did.

Scrambling through the door with Goldie sliding in behind me, I whirled around and slammed it shut so hard the etched glass vibrated.

And there she was. Right outside the door. We were face to face, eye to eye through the glass.

Zach was right. There was so much hatred emanating from her it took my breath away. Her eyes were fire. Her mouth was open, exposing a mouthful of shark teeth. She was the most terrifying thing I'd ever seen in my life.

And then she wasn't. Her face morphed into a beautiful, youthful one, a smile forming on strawberry-kissed lips. Only the deadly intent still gleaming in her eyes gave her away. Her breath fogged the glass.

I reached beside me and pushed Goldie back. Her growl turned into a whine.

The monster's hand reached out for the door handle. I suddenly couldn't remember if I'd locked it. I backed up. Her gaze moved from my face to behind me. Her hand froze. And just like that, she was gone.

I fell forward, pressing my face to the glass, scanning the yard, the street. No sign of her. No sign of the wolf or Zach either.

I felt Goldie's wet nose nudge my hand. I collapsed onto the cool marble floor, wrapping my arms around her. "What in heaven's name just happened?"

"That's what I'd like to know."

My heart sank at the sound of Daisy's voice.

Out of the frying pan and into the fire.

CHAPTER TWENTY-TWO

Leaning on Goldie for support, I pushed my depleted body off the tile.

Felix scampered out from behind Daisy and came to greet us.

While he and Goldie sniffed each other with wagging tails, I faced Daisy.

She had a small, amused smile tucked in the corner of her mouth, but her blue eyes were wary and guarded. "So, this is the second time I've found you in my house." She moved closer, her head tilting. "Are you all right? You look really pale. I mean, paler than usual."

Am I all right?

I wanted to laugh hysterically but managed to quell the urge. I was still trying to catch my breath. Lifting a thumb I motioned behind me. "Chased ... big dog."

She glanced nervously behind me, her hand fluttering to her throat. "Oh, dear." Then she placed that hand gently on my arm. "Well, come sit down. I'll have Edna get you a glass of water." She led us into the living room and left us there. "Be right back."

I collapsed onto the sofa. If she was going for a weapon to knock me off, there was nothing I could do about it now. I was too dang exhausted from all the adrenaline that had rushed through my body and was now draining away. I needed time to recover. To gather my wits. To thank my guardian stars both Goldie and I were still in one piece. Of course, I had a certain jinn to thank for that, too.

Felix stretched out against the marble fireplace. Goldie plopped down at my feet, her head resting between her paws.

I tried not to think about what could've happened if Zach hadn't intervened between her and that wolf. Then my stomach rolled as I wondered what happened to Zach. I hoped he was all right. I pushed aside that thought.

I had a more pressing problem. What was I going to say to Daisy when she asked why I was here again?

Unfortunately, I had no time to figure it out. Daisy entered the room, Edna following close behind with a tray of water glasses and cookies. Good, no gun or syringes full of deadly drugs. My luck may be changing.

"Thanks," I said weakly accepting the cold glass.

"You're welcome. Also my famous walnut cookies, straight from the oven." Edna placed the tray on the coffee table with a smile. "It's nice to have someone to feed 'em too, since I can't get this one to eat." She jerked her chin toward Daisy, who rolled her eyes.

"I'm sure they're delicious," I said absentmindedly. Out of the corner of my eye, I saw Daisy watching me closely.

"Enjoy," Edna said and left the room.

I steadied myself and met Daisy's gaze.

"So," she folded her hands together. The giant ring flashed on her finger. "To what do I owe this visit?"

My attention fell to the ring, then drifted over to the portrait of her and Barron Vanderhall. There was nothing left to do but ask. I turned back to Daisy and kept my voice soft. Wouldn't do any good to make it an accusation. "He's not your father, is he?"

My question was met with a stillness that lasted longer than I was comfortable with. After a moment, her gaze finally dropped to her ring and her shoulders fell. A sadness permeated the room. When she looked back up at me, there were tears shining in her eyes. She nodded once, rising and retrieving the photo.

I watched her cautiously, glad she was going to tell me the truth, but not knowing what the whole truth would be. Was she about to confess to murdering Peter to keep Barron from finding out about her affair with Lincoln? I glanced down at the glass of water in my hand and tried to calm my mind enough to gain control of it in case I needed a quick distraction.

She came to sit beside me, her attention still on the photo. She didn't seem threatened by my question, just sad. Still, I stayed on guard.

When she finally looked up at me, a tear broke free and rolled down her cheek. She wiped it away and placed the framed photo on the coffee table. "Yes, Barron is my husband. We met when I was trying to make it modeling in New York. I'd just lost out on a huge job with Calvin Klein and was sitting in Central Park crying and feeling completely hopeless. Not getting that job meant I couldn't afford to live in New York anymore. I'd have to go crawlin' back to my mother, a failure at nineteen. At that time I felt like my life was over." She smiled sadly at me. "You know how it is when you're a teenager ... every-thing's so dramatic. It really did feel like the end of the world."

I nodded, encouraging her to continue. "I remember."

"Anyway, Barron spotted me and came over to make sure I was all right. He listened as I poured my heart out, and we talked until the sun started to go down. I'm not sure why I opened up to a stranger like that. He just seemed to say all the right things, and I felt safe with him." She twisted the ring roughly on her finger, her face flushing. "I guess because he was so old. Like the father I never had. He offered to buy me dinner. I thought it was sweet, you know?"

I nodded.

She picked a fashion magazine up off the coffee table and began to fan herself with it. "I didn't realize at that point that his intentions weren't fatherly. I was too emotionally devastated and wrapped up in my own sureness that my life was over. My dream of being a famous model crushed."

Her fanning grew more furious. "It wasn't until he reached across the table at Vito's Italian restaurant and took my hand that I suddenly noticed the soft, loving way he was looking at me. It startled me, honestly .... and so did what he asked me next. He asked me to marry him. Can you imagine?"

She laughed then, her gaze unfocused and bewildered as she remembered that moment. "When I pulled my hand back and started to turn him down, he begged me to hear him out. I thought he was crazy. But the more he explained to me about his heart condition, and how he didn't know how much time he had left, and how he was lonely and wanted to spend his last years with someone kind and charming and beautiful ... the more I listened. The more it didn't sound so crazy.

"He played on my insecurity. He told me about his fortune and how I'd have the money to pay for the best of everything to compete in the modeling world. Plastic surgery, personal trainers, personal chefs, clothes, I could have whatever I needed to become the best version of myself." She shook her head as if chastising her younger, more naïve self and tossed the magazine back on the table. "I won't lie. That's what did it. I saw stars. I was so absolutely fixated on my dream that I didn't even stop to think about what he'd be gettin' in return."

She sighed and stared at the framed photo on the coffee table. I couldn't decipher her expression. It wasn't anger, but it was something dark. Something that I didn't dare interrupt.

I picked up a walnut cookie from the plate and shoved half of it in my mouth to keep myself quiet. She was on a roll and I didn't need to interrupt. Besides, it would be rude if I didn't try one and I must say, they were world-class cookies.

Goldie sat up and rested her chin in my lap, thinking the same thing. I broke off a small piece and fed it to her. She happily plopped back down on my feet.

Daisy finally settled back into the couch and angled herself more in my direction. She suddenly laughed bitterly, which startled me a bit. "As you can see, even with Barron's money, I didn't make it. I just wasn't pretty enough. I mean, sure I still get jobs. I just did a commercial for bathroom tissue last week."

Her face pinked. "It's not his fault. It's just not the life I imagined."

She drifted deeper inward. I tried to wait it out, but she was lost in her thoughts now.

I washed the cookie down with a sip of water and cleared my throat. "So, Daisy? What about Lincoln?"

At the mention of Lincoln's name, her attention came back to the room and to me, a smile blooming. "Lincoln." She closed her eyes and rolled his name around in her mouth like something sweet. "Lincoln Lee. Oh, Darwin, he's so amazing. My savior, really. The man who brought love into my life." She seemed startled by her own declaration. "Oh, don't get me wrong ... I've grown to care about Barron heaps over the last nine years but to be in love ... There's nothing in the world like it, is there?"

I agreed but then thought about how much pain Sylvia was in. "There are downsides, too." I caught my lip between my teeth. It was time to bring up why I was really there. I steadied myself and made sure my tone stayed soft. "Daisy?" I waited. I really needed to be looking her in the eye when I asked her this. "Daisy?"

Finally looking up at me, thoughts of Lincoln still glowing in her eyes, she said, "Yes?"

"Did you know that Peter had photos of you and Lincoln together in the parking lot of the shelter?"

She nodded. "Yes."

I blinked, taken aback. She hadn't hesitated at all to confess that knowledge. What did that mean? No time to analyze it, I had to continue. "Did Peter threaten to go to Barron with the photos if you didn't give him money for the shelter he wanted to build?"

She nodded again. "Yes."

I opened my mouth and snapped it shut, watching her warily. Did she understand she'd just confessed to having a motive to murder Peter?

She suddenly moved a hand to my knee. If she noticed me flinch, she didn't acknowledge it. "I know what you're thinking, Darwin."

If that were true, I was in big trouble.

"You think that I killed Peter because he was blackmailing me with those photos." She removed her hand and smiled at me. "I didn't. Think about it. If I was a cold-blooded killer and had access to a drug that made murder look like a heart attack, why wouldn't I just off my rich husband instead? Then the photos wouldn't matter a bit, and I could live happily ever after with the man I love."

She had a point. "So, what *did* you do when Peter threatened you with the photos?"

"Well," she stretched out her fingers and stared at the ring. "I couldn't let him tell Barron, of course. It would devastate the poor man. He's in a very fragile state right now with his health. His cardiologist has only given him months, maybe weeks to live." Her blue eyes grew moist and shiny. "I really do care about him. I want him to leave this world happy, believing that he made me happy. He deserves that at least."

She leaned back into the sofa, deflating. "I do feel guilty for betraying his trust. I begged Peter to understand this, but he was obsessed with building that doggone shelter. So, the only thing left to do was give him the million he wanted."

"So you gave him the money? A million dollars?"

Wow, Peter wasn't playing around.

She shrugged. "It's not really that much money to us. We could easily afford it. And it was going to a good cause, so I wasn't all that mad at him."

My brow furrowed. "Someone was."

"Yeah," she wrapped her arms around her thin body. An involuntary shudder ran through her. "I found that out when I went to take him the money the morning he was killed."

I blinked as that sank in. "So you were there that morning at Peter's house? The morning he was killed?"

She nodded, her pupils dilating. Shock seemed to be setting in as she remembered. "It was awful, Darwin. When I went to knock, the door just pushed open. I called into the house to let Pete know I was there." Her southern accent thickened. "But I got this feelin' runnin' up my spine that something was really, really wrong. When I walked deeper into the house, I saw him. He was just lyin' there on the floor in a tuxedo, and I ran to check his pulse, but he was already gone."

To think, at that moment, we were all in the hotel room waiting for Peter to show up, completely unaware of his demise. I felt bad for being angry with him. "Why didn't you call the police?"

Daisy's voice shook. She looked tired suddenly. "Well, I was there with a million dollars in a suitcase tryin' to keep my affair a secret. I sure wasn't going to explain to the police why I was there. Besides, I thought he'd just had a heart attack or something, he looked so peaceful and there was no sign of trauma. I figured there was nothing paramedics could do for him anyway. I didn't know he'd been murdered until you told me at Rachel's party."

I rubbed my temple, trying to put together what this meant. "So, then what did you do? Just leave?"

She shook her head, looking sheepish. "I still needed to make sure those photos of me and Lincoln didn't get out. I took his laptop and his cameras to try to keep that from happening. I did realize he could've stashed them somewhere else, but there was nothing I could do about that." She suddenly looked up. "Wait, you've seen the photos?"

I nodded. "Peter had them hidden on a thumb drive in one of the puppy's toys."

Her eyes filled with worry. "Who else has seen them?"

"The police have the thumb drive."

She tented her fingers and held them against her mouth. "Oh no, they're not going to show them to Barron, are they? It would kill him."

"I don't know. But, weren't you worried about that when Lincoln exposed your relationship to Will and me? Worried that we'd spill the beans to your husband?"

"Not really. I didn't figure you'd have any reason to talk to him. And if you did, I don't think he'd believe you anyway. He's a hard evidence kind of guy. But if someone showed him photos..." She trailed off with a shake of her head.

This time it was me who reached over and squeezed her hand. She looked so distressed, I knew then she really cared about how the news would affect her husband, even if she was in love with someone else. "Don't worry. I can talk to Will—" I froze. Everything suddenly slipped into place, giving me a little jolt.

Oh no.

"What is it?" she asked, breathless. She gripped my hand tighter. "Darwin?"

I looked at her and swallowed. "Daisy, you're not gonna want to hear what I'm about to say but please just listen with an open mind ... agreed?"

She nodded slowly, her eyes widening in fear. "Just tell me. What is it?"

"I think it was Lincoln." I nodded, now more sure of myself. "I think Lincoln killed Peter."

CHAPTER TWENTY-THREE

Daisy was shaking her head vehemently, but I saw the doubt creeping into her eyes. "He knew I'd decided to just give Peter the money. There'd be no reason for Lincoln to kill him."

I stroked Goldie, who'd sat up and rested her head in my lap again. "What about revenge? What about the fact that Peter could've decided a million dollars wasn't enough and kept asking you for more? Lincoln would've realized this was a possibility. What about just flat out anger at someone blackmailing the woman he loved?" I watched the different emotions pass over her face … denial, defensiveness, doubt, and then settle on fear.

"He had access to the drug that killed Peter at the vet clinic, Daisy. And also, you said you took Peter the money that morning alone. That means you weren't with Lincoln like you told us you were. So he doesn't actually have an alibi for the time of Peter's death. Do you know where he was that morning?"

Her voice was a whisper. Her face blotchy. "I assumed at my condo where I'd left him when I came back here to get the money from the safe. He said to tell y'all we were together to give me an alibi. So I wouldn't have to say I was at Peter's house that morning and why."

"But don't you see? You were really giving *him* an alibi."

Looking horrified, she shook her head slowly. "He wouldn't hurt Peter. He couldn't." But, I saw the possibility dawning on her and the fear growing. "Oh God. Could he have?" Her eyes grew wider. "I'm supposed to meet him for dinner tonight at BellaBrava. If he ... How can I ... do you think he'd hurt me?"

Adrenaline was pumping through my body. I really needed to talk to Will. He'd know what to do. "Daisy, where's your husband? You shouldn't be alone right now."

She stood up and started pacing. Felix watched her calmly from his position in front of the fireplace. "He's in New York, meeting with the best cardiac surgeon in the US. He left this morning."

Goldie stood and gave herself a good shake, then stared at me expectantly. She was right. We needed to skedaddle. Get Daisy to a safe place. "Okay. Here's what we're gonna do. I'm going to call Will and leave a message to fill him in. Since we know what time Lincoln will be at BellaBrava, Will can pick him up there."

If he gets my message in time.

"Meanwhile, you're coming with me. We've got to keep you out of sight and safe until Will has him in custody."

She stopped pacing and stood there biting a nail and staring at me. "Oh God, Darwin. How did it come to this?"

I stood and gave her a gentle hug. She was trembling. "It'll be all right. I promise." I mentally kicked myself. What was it with me making promises?

I really had to stop doing that. "Come on, let's get out of here."

She took a deep breath and blew it out slowly. "All right. I'll go let Edna know she's gonna have Felix for a little while. I'll meet you in the car."

I stepped out of her house cautiously looking for any sign of the crazy woman or the wolf.

The street was quiet, just some white Ibis poking around the yard and a black Mercedes rolling by. Resting a hand on Goldie, I whispered, "All clear, girl." Still, I found myself power-walking to the car, trying to outrun the chill creeping up my spine. Letting Goldie jump in back first, I quickly slid in after her and slammed the door.

Praying for a message from Will, I dug my phone out of my abandoned straw bag.

Yes! He had tried to call. Finally!

"Will!" Relief flooded over me at the sound of his voice.

He was okay. Thank heavens.

"Where are you, Darwin?" The relief faded as I heard the strain in his voice.

I glanced over as Daisy opened the car door and slid into the passenger seat. She clutched a flowered travel bag and still seemed in shock.

I gave her a reassuring smile and pointed to the phone, mouthing, "It's Will."

Then, trying to keep the worry from creeping into my own voice, I said to Will, "I'm just about to leave Daisy's house. I have so much to tell you but first, we really have to get out of here and get her to a safe place."

"Daisy's with you now?"

I busied myself putting the top up on the car in case the crazy fish-woman was still lurking around. "Yes."

"I'm not on speaker, am I?"

"Nope."

"Listen, Darwin. I couldn't get a hold of Mr. Vanderhall, so I went ahead and interviewed Sassy White at the station. She provided proof that the van actually has been broken down so there's no motive for blackmail. She also gave us a second alibi for earlier that morning from Sunny's, the place she'd stopped for breakfast. It checked out so she's no longer a suspect. But then I got some interesting news. Our team dug up Daisy's maiden name which is not Vanderhall like she told us. Vanderhall is her married name. Barron Vanderhall is actually her husband, not her father."

"Yeah, I know."

"You know? Did she tell you?" Will asked.

"Yes."

"Then the question is why would she lie to you in the first place? Something seems off. I need to talk to her again, and I don't like that you're alone with her."

Daisy was shifting uncomfortably in the seat, clutching her bag and watching me intently. "We should go," she whispered.

I nodded to her and held up a finger.

I was starting to feel waves of anxiety from Daisy. They were raising my own. Goldie's hot breath was on my shoulder. She probably felt it, too. I flipped the air conditioning higher and put the car in drive, my thoughts racing.

As I pulled around Daisy's circle drive and headed back toward town, I had an idea. "Will, remember that

... safe house you told me about? The hotel room you guys have reserved for ... special cases?"

"Yes," Will said.

"Can we stay there while you go pick up Lincoln? We think he might be the one who poisoned Peter. He wasn't actually with Daisy the morning Peter was killed, so he doesn't have an alibi. It's a long story— I'll tell you later. But right now he's supposed to meet Daisy for dinner at BellaBrava. You can pick him up there for questioning."

I glanced over at Daisy. Her gaze was fixed on the road.

Will was silent for a moment. Then he said, "That means Daisy doesn't have an alibi either, so yeah, good idea. I'll call ahead to the hotel and arrange it. Just go to the front desk, and ask for Detective Blake's room. They'll know what to do."

I crossed the Snell Isle bridge. The sky was beginning to glow orange beneath the belly of heavy, gray clouds. "Thanks, Will."

"And Darwin ... Be careful."

"Don't worry about me. Just find Lincoln."

CHAPTER TWENTY-FOUR

Daisy stood at the window, between the half-drawn curtains. We were on the third floor in an unremarkable hotel room. Flowered bedspread, dark dresser with a TV, tropical bird prints hanging on pale peach walls. It smelled musty and faintly of Pine-Sol.

My head rested against the dark wood headboard. My arm was draped over Goldie, who was pressed up against my side, her eyes half-closed.

The blue glow of Daisy's phone reflected off of the glass. She was texting someone. Her husband?

I wondered but didn't ask. I was bone tired. Drained. Whatever happened now would just have to play itself out. For Sylvia's sake, I hoped we were in the final act. Time was up.

My phone sat on the nightstand to my right, beside a room service menu and a notepad and pen with the hotel logo. I had already texted Will that we were here and had also texted Mallory that I was safe so they wouldn't worry.

"What if Lincoln doesn't show up at BellaBrava?" Daisy said, turning. "Maybe he's already skipped town, and we'll never know why he did it. Would the police still pursue him in another country?"

Her questions confused my already tired brain. Why would he skip town? He had no idea we were on to him. I pulled my knees into my chest and stared at her.

She wouldn't ... would she? I wanted to ask her if she'd warned Lincoln, but just then a light knock sounded on the door.

Her body stiffened.

"Oh no," she whispered. Rushing across the threadbare carpet, she was at the door before I could warn her not to open it.

Too late.

She flung the door open. A defeated moan escaped her throat. "Why did you come here?"

I scrambled up as Lincoln strolled into the room and shut the door behind him. He glanced at me and Goldie on the bed. We stared back at him. He was wearing jeans, a green "adopt-don't-shop" t-shirt and a very worried expression. Daisy *must* have warned him. It was the only explanation.

She moved to stand in front of Lincoln. Her fists were clenched at her sides, her face reddening. Tears were welling up in her eyes. "Why on earth did you come here?"

He lifted his hands up to her cheeks and, gently cupping her face, he kissed her. Her body softened as the kiss melted away her anger.

When he broke the kiss, he said, "Because I'm not leaving without you. We do this together."

"Oh, Lincoln, you fool." She wrapped her arms around him, pressing her cheek into his chest. "You could've gotten away clean. Started a new life."

"I don't want a life without you."

I lowered my feet to the floor and wrapped my arms protectively around Goldie. "I don't mean to interrupt the lovefest here, but Daisy ... did you warn

Lincoln that Will was looking for him? Doesn't that kind of defeat the purpose of us being here hiding from him?"

They shared a look and then Lincoln bowed his head. Daisy brushed a dark wave off his forehead and lifted his chin. "All right. Together."

Lincoln slid a desk chair up to the bed and sat down, facing me. Daisy slipped onto his lap, her arm draped over his shoulder.

I watched them expectantly.

Lincoln rubbed a hand roughly over his face and let his dark eyes meet mine. I was surprised by the sincerity I saw there. "Darwin, I didn't kill Peter, and I don't want anyone else to get hurt. All I want is for me and Daisy to be able to leave this room, and for you to give us time to get to the airport before you alert your detective boyfriend. I already have a flight booked for us both. Two hours. That's all I'm asking."

I dug my fingers into Goldie's fur for comfort. "If you didn't kill Peter, why are you running?"

He glanced at Daisy. He didn't mean to, it was a reflex, but it told me all I needed to know.

I shifted my focus. "So, you killed him, Daisy. Why? Over the photos of you and Lincoln together?"

She sighed. Her voice was barely a whisper when she answered me. "Yes."

I shook my head in disbelief. "I don't understand. Like you said, it would've been easier to just kill your husband. A heart attack wouldn't have even been questioned at his age with his heart condition."

She shrugged and at least had the decency to look remorseful. "Actually, while he does have a heart condition, it's not quite as serious as I made it out to be. The old geezer's probably gonna outlive me. He's in New York on business." Then she pressed her lips together and dropped her head.

I waited but she wasn't going to say anything more.

"I see." I was trying to keep my expression as calm and neutral as possible. Inside I was screaming *I see … but I still don't understand.*

Lincoln watched me for a few seconds and then said, "I'll explain everything on one condition. You have to agree not to alert your boyfriend until after we've caught our flight. Give us the two-hour head start I've asked for."

Daisy looked up at me. Her blue eyes were swimming with regret. "She'll never agree to that. She's straight as an arrow."

"I am not!" I gave her my most indignant look. This had to be believable. *Negotiate, Darwin.* That's what anyone considering his offer would do. "He just hasn't made the right offer yet." I mentally patted myself on the back.

Her expression changed. She sat up straighter on his lap, a bit of hope pushing aside the regret. "And what would the right offer be?"

"Well." I crossed my arms, trying to look more confident than I felt. I uncrossed them and crossed my legs. With a huff, Goldie rested her head in my lap. As I stroked her ears, my gaze slid from Lincoln's stoic face to Daisy's waiting one. Then it swept down to her hand.

Yes. That's it.

I motioned to her hand with my chin. "I want the ring."

She glanced down and then back up at me with a questioning smirk. She held up her hand. "This ring?

You want it? Why? You don't strike me as poor. I'm finding it hard to believe money would be enough motivation for you to let us get away."

She knew me better than I thought. "It's not about the money, and it's not for my sake. It's for Peter's and all the animals that'll be saved when his dream shelter gets built. It's about making things right. Fulfilling your end of the bargain you made with him. Don't you want to make things right?"

She nodded, accepting that as a believable motivation. "Done." She slipped the ring off of her finger and held it out to me on her palm. "Don't settle for anything less than a million. That should get you enough to buy the land. The rest will be up to you. Like I told you, I don't mind my money going to a good cause."

I took the ring from her with shaking fingers and closed my sweaty palm around it. Its weight made the situation I was in suddenly all too real.

Don't think, Darwin. Just keep going.

"Okay. Now I believe you owe me the truth."

They glanced at each other and Daisy slipped her now bare hand into Lincoln's. "All right. The truth." Daisy's gaze drifted toward the window. Lincoln gave her hand a squeeze of encouragement.

She moved her attention back to me, and I actually felt sorry for her in that moment. There was so much grief etched in the lines around her eyes and mouth. So much wild sorrow shining in her watery blue eyes. I knew whatever she was about to tell me was not going to be the confession of a cold-blooded killer, but a story about how her life decisions went terribly, horribly wrong.

"The truth is, when Peter tried to blackmail me with the photos, he didn't realize one thing. Even though I was married to a wealthy man—and it's true that a million dollars is nothing to Barron—I didn't have access to any of the money. I couldn't pay Peter if I wanted to. Barron had made me sign a pre-nup stating that I wouldn't have any control over his money, that everything I spent would have to be approved by him. But that's not the reason I had to kill Peter. Also in the pre-nup, it stated that I would inherit none of Barron's money unless we'd been married for at least ten years before he passed. That's why I had to kill Peter. We're eleven months shy of that." She threw a hand up in frustration. "I begged Peter to wait a year, but he refused. He'd just shouted some statistic at me about how many animals would be dead in a year. Ones he could've saved."

My mouth was so dry, but I had to keep her talking. "So, that's why you couldn't just kill your husband instead of Peter. Because you would lose all that inheritance?"

Poor Peter. Yes, blackmailing Daisy was wrong but … the timing made it even sadder. In eleven months he wouldn't have been able to blackmail her at all, and he would still be alive. Heck, she would've probably given him the money after that.

"Yes and I wasn't about to let that happen. I couldn't. I wasted my twenties with that man. Almost a decade gone. My youth. I deserved to at least have the money he dangled in front of me to bind me to him." Her body was shaking now.

A wave of her rage washed over me. It startled me as it disturbed the numbness I'd been feeling.

With a deep breath, I pushed it aside and tried to keep her calm. "I understand, Daisy, and it wasn't right of Peter to blackmail you. Go on. What exactly happened the morning he died?"

Her expression changed to one of horror. Her face paled. "I honestly didn't know." She squeezed her eyes shut and shook her head slowly. Lincoln tightened his arm around her waist. "It was really terrible."

When she spoke again, her voice was strained. "I didn't know how the drug would affect him. Lincoln and I hadn't really talked about it passed the point of it just being a quick death that would look like a heart attack."

"I'm sorry," he whispered to her. "I would have warned you. But, we weren't ready to use it yet."

I glanced at Lincoln. "This is the sux you stole from Southern Cross where you work?"

He nodded. "Yes."

Again, I was struck by how sincere and full of regret he seemed. I would never peg him as someone willing to kill for what he wanted. "But, I don't understand one thing. How did it go missing *after* Peter's death and not before?"

Lincoln's leg was shaking now. He was getting nervous. Or antsy. "I'd been siphoning off a bit at a time from other vials for months. I had to get enough to … you know."

"Kill someone," I finished for him.

He cringed. "Yeah. So the theft went undetected the first time. But since Daisy used what I'd got on Peter, we needed another dose for our original plan. I got impatient and took a whole vial, hoping I could cover it up during inventory."

Did Lincoln realize, even if he didn't kill Peter himself, stealing the drug made him an accessory, and he'd probably get just as much time? Such a wasted life.

"What was your original plan?" I asked.

Daisy jumped in. "You have to understand, Darwin, I couldn't live with that man a day past the decade I had to. And I would barely get enough to live off of if I divorced him. The only way I was getting what I deserved was if he died. So, it was to be my anniversary present to myself. Freedom."

Goldie jumped off the bed and stretched. The empty space where she'd just been pressing against my side suddenly made me feel vulnerable. I had to wrap this up so they could leave.

"Let me make sure I got this straight. Y'all planned to kill Barron with the sux Lincoln stole, but only after the ten years was up so you'd receive his inheritance?"

"Yes," Daisy said. "And Lincoln and I were going to have the life we deserved ... together." Her mouth tightened in anger. "Of course now, we won't have all his money but," she turned and her expression softened. "I took enough of my jewelry for us to live comfortably on for a while, and all that matters now is we'll be together."

He pulled her closer in to him. "Always."

This was just all so sad. For everyone involved. I glanced behind them.

Goldie had gone to lay by the door.

Yeah, I'm anxious to get out of here, too, girl.

I had to get Daisy back on track and finish her story. "So then Daisy, you went to Peter's house that morning ... and you had the sux with you?"

"Yeah but you know, just as a last resort type of thing. Honest. I guess it gave me a sense of control, some way to stop him if he refused to listen to me. There really was no plan but that. I thought I could reason with him. He'd always been so nice to me. I thought once I'd explained to him that I didn't have access to Barron's money, and if he'd just wait a year I'd gladly give it to him.

"But he didn't believe me. He got really fired up." Her hand gestures grew animated. "Like face turning purple, eyes bulging angry. Said he was going to Barron right after he was done shooting the wedding he had that morning."

She shifted on Lincoln's lap. "I panicked. When he turned his back on me, I just jammed the needle in his neck and pressed the plunger. It was so easy. I couldn't believe I did it. The look on his face when he whirled around. Confusion ... then anger ... then ... when he felt his muscles begin to seize ... fear."

Her hand fluttered up to her mouth. "He collapsed on the floor. It only took seconds before he was staring up at me unable to blink, and then finally unable to breathe. I could tell he was still in there. He was begging me for help with his eyes, from inside that frozen body. And that poor little puppy kept scratching at his arm and barking. Trying to get him to get up, I guess. I couldn't take it. I had to put the poor thing in his carrier before I left."

She shivered. "I've had nightmares ever since."

So, she did put Petey in his carrier the morning Peter died. My vision was of the killer's hand, and I was now holding the ring I saw, listening to the killer's confession.

I swallowed my own horror, gritting my teeth. When I got my reaction under control, I managed to ask the one thing I wanted to know for myself. "Are you even a little bit remorseful, Daisy?"

She jerked her head up. "Well, of course. I feel awful. Peter didn't deserve to die. If I could go back and do it all again, I would've just offed Barron instead, his fortune be damned. I mean, in the end I didn't get it anyway, did I? Lincoln and I will survive. We'll be fine."

So, after all that, the one thing she would change was to kill her husband instead of Peter? Unbelievable.

"I guess that's it then. Goldie, come here, girl." I patted the bed. Reluctantly, she came over and jumped up beside me, looking a little confused. "Y'all better get out of here. You've got a plane to catch."

"Yes, we should go." Daisy stood up and retrieved her bag.

Lincoln was still watching me.

I wasn't sure he trusted me to keep my word, but his only other option was to tie me up or otherwise dispose of me. He didn't seem up for any more violence.

"Thank you, Darwin. I hope you don't think too badly of Daisy."

He was still thinking of her. I felt bad for him. "It's not for me to judge."

He nodded once, stood and moved to the door.

Daisy turned back to me one last time when she reached his side. "You gave us your word. Remember, no calls for two hours."

I nodded. "I never go back on my word."

Daisy smiled and nodded. "I know. You're a good person. Goodbye, Darwin."

"Goodbye, Daisy." I held on to Goldie's collar as they opened the door.

"Police! Don't move!"

Daisy dropped her bag with a gasp. They both lifted their hands slowly.

"Get down on the ground!" an officer commanded.

I guess the gun convinced them to comply.

Will rushed into the room as three officers handcuffed Daisy and Lincoln and lifted them off the ground.

He pulled me up into his arms. "You okay?"

I nodded but a tear slipped down my face. "The way Peter died..." I whispered into his tie.

"I know." He kissed the top of my head. "But they will pay for it. Because of your quick thinking." He stroked my hair with one hand and reached down and gave Goldie a pat with the other. "Bringing Daisy here was pure genius."

I pulled away and wiped at my eyes. One of the officers was reaching around the lamp on the dresser. "Did you get it all?" I asked.

"Yes, ma'am." He shot me a smile and held up a small listening device. "Good work."

"Glad you remembered about the drug sting we had set up here," Will said. "We've got their whole confession, both audio and," he pointed up to the smoke detector, "on camera."

I opened my hand. I'd been squeezing the ring so tightly, the large diamond had left an imprint on my palm. "Oh, here's Daisy's ring. The one from my vision."

Will stared at it for a moment and then folded my hand back around it. "Daisy gave it to you to build Peter's shelter. She said that on camera. No one will dispute that. Build the shelter, Darwin. Give Peter's story a better ending."

I choked, the emotion overwhelming me as I nodded. It felt like the right thing to do.

CHAPTER TWENTY-FIVE

The Vinoy Resort's main wedding venue was already booked. But like Frankie always said, "Money talks." And she had enough of it to talk her way right into reserving the pool area so Sylvia and Landon could say *I do* under a sky full of stars. She'd also managed to salvage the wedding cake, have the resort agree to cater it, find a new photographer and dazzle us with the tropical fairytale ambiance she'd created.

I'd overhead some of the guests commenting on what a beautiful set-up she'd pulled off after the original disaster. I had to agree after getting a sneak peek of it myself.

There were hundreds of floating tea candles in the pool, along with red rose petals sprinkled on the surface amongst them. Strings of twinkling white lights had been wrapped around the palm trees like candy canes.

To the right were clusters of round tables covered in white tablecloths and sporting fat, red rose and candle centerpieces. The chairs had been draped in elegant white banquet covers with red satin bows affixed to the backs. Soothing piano music drifted over the guests, along with the sound of rain from the glistening sheet of water flowing into the pool from the back wall fountain. The whole thing just whispered peace, love and harmony.

I had to hand it to her. Will and I may have solved a murder in a week, but as far as impossible tasks went, Frankie had won hands down.

From our position on the outdoor patio below the final set of stairs, the bridal party heard the piano music pause and then start "Ave Maria," signaling it was time.

Sylvia's cousins descended on her one last time with hugs and squeals, before they made their way up the stairs.

I shared a teary-eyed grin with Sylvia. It was happening. Finally. I felt like I could breathe deeply for the first time in a week. I couldn't even imagine the relief she was feeling.

"We did it," I whispered, being careful not to squash her bouquet as I hugged her and struggled to hold back tears. "And you are the most beautiful bride on the planet."

"And you are the best friend a girl could ask for." Her tears did fall, but luckily her makeup was waterproof. "Thank you for everything you did to make this happen."

"Yeah well, when you asked me to be your Maid of Honor, I didn't know the duties included solving a murder. But guess it wasn't much worse than sitting through that pedicure." We shared a laugh and another hug. I glanced over my shoulder one last time before ascending the stairs. "Just remember to name your firstborn after me."

Her deep chuckle followed me as I made the short climb and emerged onto the pool deck. A warm breeze cooled the back of my neck. Following the white runner along the pool, I walked slowly toward the altar, glad I had opted to go barefoot this time. Much more comfortable and much less chance of spraining my ankle again or falling into the pool.

The groomsmen were waiting there beside a beaming Landon. His hand resting on Mage, panting at his side.

Will held my gaze as I walked down the aisle. He winked at me as I took my place beside the cousins, causing me to blush. I couldn't help but imagine it was our wedding day to see what that felt like.

Pretty terrifying, actually.

The piano music shifted smoothly into The Wedding March. Chairs rustled as the guests stood, turning toward the back in anticipation.

Sylvia emerged looking like the quintessential princess bride in her cloud of white taffeta and crystal tiara. She was glowing. Her eyes were locked onto Landon and the closer she got to him, the wider her smile got.

I'd never seen her so happy. In fact, I'd never experienced such an assault of happiness before. A tsunami-like wave carried pure bliss through me. My skin tingled. The lights brightened. The air smelled sweeter. It was euphoric.

The ceremony began with Sylvia and Landon holding hands and staring into each other's eyes. I was pretty sure they weren't aware of anything else around them.

"Do you, Landon Stark, take Sylvia Alvarez to be your lawfully wedded wife, to have and to hold, to honor and treasure in sickness and in health, in good times and bad, to love and to cherish always?"

Tears and certainty glistened in Landon's eyes as he said, "I do."

Mage shoved his nose in between their hands and they both chuckled, giving him a reassuring pet before turning their attention back to each other.

As the officiator continued, Sylvia's mother sniffled loudly in the front row and blew her nose into a handkerchief. I wasn't sure if hers were happy tears or not.

When we'd handed her a copy of the police report, showing the arrests of Daisy Beaumont and Lincoln Lee for Peter's murder, she'd gone still and pale. I thought she was going to pass out. She kept saying '*impossível*' over and over. I think she was actually disappointed.

Today, I was willing to give her the benefit of the doubt.

"Do you, Sylvia Alvarez, take Landon Stark to be your lawfully wedded husband, to have and to hold, to honor and treasure in sickness and in health, in good times and bad, to love and to cherish always?"

Sylvia looked radiant as she said, "I do."

Another rush of emotion washed over me. It was hot and all-consuming. Leaning forward a bit, my gaze found Will.

He was so handsome and such a good man. *Did I feel that strongly about him?*

He smiled softly at me. One thing's for sure, that smile did light me up inside.

The officiator finished. "I now pronounce you man and wife. You may kiss the bride."

Sylvia squealed. Landon swept her up into his arms and smothered her with a long kiss. Mage barked.

The guests burst out in applause. Frankie whistled.

Sylvia's mother blew her nose loudly.

Piano music accompanied the beaming bride and groom back down the aisle, the guests blowing bubbles around them. It took them awhile to make it through the gauntlet as everyone wanted their turn to hug the newlyweds and give their congratulations.

Will and I finally caught up to them. The new photographer was taking photos of the happy couple with some of the guests. We got in there and got a few of us with them, too. This was definitely a day I wanted to remember. The week before, not so much.

Landon squeezed me in a tight hug. "Thank you, Darwin. You are a true friend and we won't forget what you did for us."

I looked into his eyes and nodded. There were no words adequate enough to express my own joy and relief. "Just take care of our girl."

"You know it. She's my world." He turned his attention to Will. "Hey, I owe you one, Detective."

Will ducked his head self-consciously. "Consider it a wedding present. I didn't get you anything."

When Will and Landon were done doing the man-hug-back-pat thing, Landon grinned at us both. "I know I'm the magician here, but you guys really did work some magic this week."

I shrugged. "Like I told Sylvia, naming your firstborn after me should settle us up fair and square."

Mage barked sharply and pawed at Landon's jacket.

We all laughed as Landon gave Mage's ears a good scratch. "Yeah, I don't think we should mention babies in front of this guy just yet."

The sound of conversation, laughter and champagne bottles being popped filled the warm night air. I looked for my sisters, but they seemed to have disappeared into the crowd. Oh well, I'd find them eventually.

There was one more thing I had to do tonight. I scanned the area and found my target.

Placing a hand on Will's arm, I said, "There's someone I need to speak to, I'll find you in a minute."

He kissed me softly. "I'll get us a drink."

* * *

"Hey."

Zach's gaze was fixed on a tea candle floating in the pool. His hands were shoved deep in the pockets of his black slacks. The sleeves of his dress shirt had been rolled and pushed up on his arms. He didn't look up as he whispered, "Hello, Darwin."

I fidgeted with my ring then shifted my weight restlessly. I wasn't sure what to say. He had saved Goldie's life and probably mine, as well. Again. "Thank you" just didn't seem adequate.

Why did I feel so awkward around him? No, not awkward maybe just more aware of myself. It was getting annoying.

I cleared my throat. "Great wedding, huh?"

Finally, he lifted his head and turned his body to face me. He took a deep breath and blew it out slowly. Tiny red embers danced in his eyes, betraying his calm exterior. He nodded once. "Yes. Glad everything worked out for them."

I took a shaky step back as I felt his heat encircle me. Then I gasped as pool water sloshed over my feet.

Startled, we both glanced down.

The tea lights were pitching wildly, some already snuffed out as the disturbance settled back down.

One of the red rose petals was stuck to my bare toe. I squeezed my eyes shut for a moment, too embarrassed to look back up at him.

His deep chuckle reverberated in my own lungs. A rush of anger gave me the strength to face him. I straightened my shoulders and looked up into his face. "I'm so glad my lack of control amuses you."

Zach's gaze was resting lightly on my mouth. "I'm not laughing at you, Darwin. I'm just amused by the absurdity of our situation." He looked into my eyes. "And your denial."

Ignoring the ache that had begun in my chest, I stuttered, "Denial? I told you I'm practicing."

He took a step closer, eliminating the space between us.

I gasped and hated myself for it. Clutching the dress material at my thigh to keep from reaching out, I steadied myself against the electric waves of desire now pulsing through my body. I felt unmoored. Unpredictable.

What was happening to me? Was this some sort of jinn magick?

Zach smiled softly and then lowered his mouth to my ear. His hot breath against my skin almost did me in. The world was spinning and my focus had shrunk down to a pinpoint. Him. Only him. I could feel my resolve faltering.

"That's not the denial I'm talking about."

I tried to swallow but my mouth was too dry.

Mercifully, he stepped back, and with the space that had opened up between us, my senses rushed back in.

He watched me for a moment and then nodding like he'd answered his own question, he changed the subject. "We'll talk about the incident on Snell Isle later. Right now, go celebrate with your friends ...you've earned it." He turned abruptly and walked away, but over his shoulder he called back, "And you're welcome."

I watched him round the pool and then my attention caught on a still figure standing on the other end of the pool. My stomach cramped.

Will was there, staring in my direction, holding two glasses of champagne. His eyes were unreadable from this distance, but I could imagine what Zach and I must've looked like that close, staring into each other's eyes.

Why hadn't I been more aware of that? Yeah, I knew why.

CHAPTER TWENTY-SIX

Sighing, I dropped my head and went to try to explain. I stood in front of him, feeling his anger and betrayal. I wanted to crawl under a rock. "Will, I—"

"Not tonight." He cut me off, handing me one of the glasses. "Tonight, it's about Sylvia and Brandon." He clinked my glass. "And celebrating getting justice for Peter Vanek."

I nodded, suddenly not in the mood to celebrate.

Mallory showed up at that moment and threaded her arm through mine. She'd smuggled Petey into the wedding in a large purse, but now he was happily tucked in the crook of her arm, wearing a tiny tux and bow tie.

Where in the world was she getting these outfits? She must have raided the boxes in the storage room.

"Come on, Sylvia's about to toss the bouquet. Would be a shame if you missed out on that." She winked at Will, oblivious to the tension between us.

I cringed and, shooting Will an apologetic look, let her lead me away. "You really have to stop carrying Petey around, Mal. He's got his own legs for a reason."

"What for? You know this is the destiny of all tiny dogs." She shared a flirtatious smile with a young man as we walked past him. I rolled my eyes.

Destiny. What a loaded word. Like the universe has some magical plan already mapped out for our lives. I would much rather believe in free will. Believe that we have a say in who and what we allow into our lives and what path our lives would take.

But, then I thought of Zach and how out of control I felt around him. Like my body had its own ideas about what it wanted.

I shook off that thought as Mallory yanked me into the group of excited, single women gathered for their shot at catching the bouquet … and maybe the next marriage proposal. When Mallory released my hand, I slipped into the back of the bunch.

For the next hour I watched everyone else having a good time, dancing and laughing under the stars, while I felt completely out of sync and out of sorts.

Frankie had tried to cheer me up at one point when she found me sitting on the edge of the pool alone, soaking my feet in the water for comfort. With her arm around me and her own bare feet dangling in the pool, we talked about ideas for Peter's shelter. She was sure wherever he was, he was grateful that something good was going to come out of his murder.

I tilted my head back and looked up at the cloudless sky. Clusters of stars burned and twinkled above us. "I think we should call it the Peter Vanek Animal Rescue."

"I think that's a great idea, sugar." She squeezed my shoulder. "I may know nothing about management or accounting, but you know I put together a heck of a fundraiser. We'll have Pete's shelter up and running in no time."

"I do know. What would I do without you?" Sighing, I leaned my head on her shoulder. She smelled like lemons and champagne. Then I sat back up. "Oh, remind me to put you in touch with this rich model I met ... Bianca Rubio. She returned Will's call this morning, and he told her everything. Apparently, she'd been in love with Peter for months, and he'd finally asked her out. They were supposed to go to dinner the day he died."

"Ouch," Frankie whispered.

"I know. Anyway, she never told him she had money. Said she wanted to make sure he wasn't using her to build the shelter he was obsessed with. But, she does want to give more than the five-hundred she pledged on the Fund Me page, so be sure to give her a call."

"All right, I will. That's sad, though. Seems Peter just missed out on a great life," Frankie said.

"Seems he did." I suddenly had the urge to sneak out of the wedding early. Being at home, snuggling in bed with Goldie, hiding from the rest of the world was the only place I wanted to be right now.

But my southern manners wouldn't let me cut out early, so I stood and helped Frankie up instead. "Come on, let's go see if there's any of that lemon cake left."

While I was piling a piece of cake on a plastic plate, applause broke out behind me. I looked up in time to see a half dozen doves gliding above my head. Must've been one of Landon's magic tricks.

Glancing over at the crowd, I noticed Sylvia's mother had a huge grin on her face, and she was still clapping. Frankie and I shared a surprised smile. My aching heart warmed at bit. Maybe Landon would win her over after all.

Turning back to the table, I shoved a forkful of cake in my mouth. Forget diamonds, cake was definitely a girl's best friend.

"May I have this dance?"

Startled by the voice in my ear, I whirled around, fork still stuck in my mouth.

Will.

His blue eyes were glassy and brimming with emotion. Hurt? Anger? Affection? His white tux shirt was untucked, sleeves rolled up, bowtie nowhere in sight. He was a mess. I nodded and tried to swallow the sticky cake and the lump in my throat.

Slipping an arm around my waist, he led me over near the piano. Then he pulled me against him and we began to sway slowly together to the music. It wasn't jazz anymore. More melancholy, like end of the evening lounge music. It fit my mood like a glove.

After a moment, I felt a tiny rumble in his chest ... a groan or a sigh. He pressed a kiss into my hair. His voice broke as he whispered, "I don't want to fight."

Closing my eyes, I pressed my cheek firmly against his chest. "Me either."

He stopped swaying. I lifted my chin up to face him. Yep, definitely hurt brewing in his eyes. But also tenderness. Slipping a hand behind my neck, he lowered his mouth near mine. Scotch permeated his breath. He held my gaze as he added, "And I don't want to lose you."

Then he kissed me. Soft at first. Then like a man drowning.

I melted into him. Leaning my forehead on his chest after the kiss, I wanted to reassure him that he wouldn't. Couldn't ever lose me. But, there was that one tiny raw spot in my heart. He wasn't comfortable with my psychic connection to animals. And he'd taken a "don't ask, don't tell" stance on my water magick. Would he eventually accept all of me?

I lifted my chin again and our eyes met. I guess only time would tell.

I cupped his flushed cheek. "I do love you, Will."

Relief surfaced in his smile and he wrapped me tightly in his arms. "I love you, too."

* * *

By the time Mallory, Willow and I made the short trek back to the townhouse from the Vinoy, it was past ten thirty, and the moon was a pale watermark in the dark sky. Low clouds had moved in, obscuring most of the stars.

We were all holding our shoes and our stomachs—leaning against each other like we used to do as kids—as we strolled down Beach Drive. Petey was snoozing in Mallory's purse, passed out from all the attention. Probably having a belly full of the chicken meatballs she kept sneaking him all night didn't help, either.

"You and Will okay?" Willow asked suddenly. "I saw him leave early."

"Yeah. He was just tired. Long week."

Willow glanced at me, but she let it go.

Unfortunately, Mallory didn't. "Did his abandoning you early have anything to do with Zach Faraday?"

"Mal," Willow warned her.

Mallory glanced over at her. "What? I'm just saying. I'd be upset if a jinn was lurking around my girlfriend all the time, too."

"He doesn't lurk," I snapped, surprising myself.

Both of them gave me a sharp look.

We stopped to check for traffic before crossing Fourth Avenue. Live music drifted toward us from The Moon Under Water restaurant.

Zach. The cause of so much confusion in my life. But I was too drained to deny my affection for him right now. Too tired to fight and too grateful to want to. Aside from my family, Zach was the only person in the world who knew and accepted everything about me.

We crossed the road.

"Besides, if he hadn't been there in front of Daisy's house last night, I don't even want to think about what could've happened to Goldie. He probably saved her life. He's not a bad guy and frankly, I think the fact that you keep bringing up his jinn side is kind of prejudiced, Mal."

She stiffened beside me and withdrew her arm from mine. "Geeze. Sorry," she mumbled.

I felt bad for hurting her feelings, but at that moment I knew one thing for sure. I did want Zach in my life. I did. Despite what the fallout would be with Will and despite Grandma Winters' warning to stay away from him, I had a right to choose who I wanted in my life. "He's my friend, so I suggest y'all get used to him being around, and that's all I'm going to say on the matter."

"Fine," Mallory said.

Willow stayed silent but she did give my hand a squeeze. I took that as a sign of support.

After we'd passed a guitarist entertaining a small crowd of diners at the sidewalk tables, I changed the subject. "Good news though. Frankie says she can get Daisy's ring into an auction next month where we can get top dollar for it. I've decided to call it the Peter Vanek Animal Rescue, what do y'all think?"

"Love it," Willow said, giving my arm a pat. "It's a good way to honor him."

We passed the Hooker Tea Company, and I had a sudden craving for some of their strawberry lemonade tea, which I was out of. I was making a mental note to pick up some tomorrow when Mallory suddenly sighed.

"I wish I could stay here and help with the shelter. It'd be so much fun."

I stopped in my tracks. My heart did a little tumble of excitement. "Well, why can't you?" I asked, quite serious. "I'd love to have you move here. Both of you. You know I have the room."

Mallory blinked, glancing from me to Willow. I could see her struggling with the idea and the many excuses I'm sure were popping up like bubbles in her mind. Finally, her green eyes widened with excitement. "Well, why not? Lucky's happy here." Her excitement grew as she peered into her bag at the sleeping puppy. "You could even keep Petey, since we'd be here to help take care of him. Willow, what do you think?"

Willow rested her head on my shoulder. I could feel the weight of her fatigue. "And leave Mom all alone? I'd feel too guilty." She must've seen the same disappointment in Mallory's face as I did. She quickly added, "But I don't like the idea of leaving Darwin here alone with that fish-woman stalking her, either.

So, let's talk about it more in the morning, okay? When we're all not too tired to think straight."

Mallory nodded, satisfied. She gave me a hopeful smile.

I was thinking about Sandy as we rounded the outside wall of Darwin's Pet Boutique—about how I might even be able to adopt her if my sisters lived here—when my sisters suddenly stopped in their tracks. I looked up.

There, waiting outside the townhome's iron gate, was a sight that sent a chill of dread up my spine.

"Grandma Winters?" Mallory cried. "What are you doing here?"

She stood and eyed us all, her expression darker than I'd ever seen it. "It's time for us to have a chat about your father, girls."

12735021R00133

Made in the USA
Monee, IL
29 September 2019